The Queen of the Dying Light

Terry Deary

Illustrated by Hemesh Alles

Dolphin Paperbacks

For Linda Anderson, with thanks for support
when it really mattered

First published in Great Britain in 1999
as a Dolphin paperback
by Orion Children's Books
a division of the Orion Publishing Group Ltd
Orion House
5 Upper St Martin's Lane
London WC2H 9EA

A catalogue record for this book is available from the British Library

Printed in Great Britain by Clays Ltd, St Ives plc

ISBN 1 85881 525 8 (pb)

Contents

All chapter titles are quotations from *All's Well that End's Well*. This play was written by William Shakespeare in 1602, the year of the events in this story. It is a play about faithful love and disloyalty.

The Marsden Family

WILLIAM MARSDEN *The narrator*
The youngest member of the family. Training to be a knight like his ancestors, although the great days of knighthood are long gone. His father insists on it and Great-Uncle George hopes for it. But he'd rather be an actor like the travelling players he has seen in the city. He can dream.

Grandmother **LADY ELEANOR MARSDEN**
She was a lady-in-waiting to Queen Anne Boleyn. After seeing the fate of her mistress she came to distrust royalty, but continued to work for them when she was called upon. Behind her sharp tongue there is a sharper brain. She is wiser than she looks.

Grandfather **SIR CLIFFORD MARSDEN**
He was a soldier in Henry VIII's army where (Grandmother says) the batterings softened his brain. Sir Clifford is the head of the family although he does not manage the estate these days – he simply looks after the money it makes. He is well known for throwing his gold around like an armless man.

Great-Uncle **SIR GEORGE SULGRAVE**
A knight who lost his lands and now lives with his stepsister, Grandmother Marsden. He lives in the past and enjoys fifty-year-old stories as much as he enjoys fifty-year-old wine. He never lets the truth stand in the way of a good story.

SIR JAMES MARSDEN *William's father*
He runs the Marsden estate and is magistrate for the district. He believes that, without him, the forces of evil would take over the whole of the land. This makes him a harsh and humourless judge. As a result he is as popular as the plague.

LADY MARSDEN *William's mother*
She was a lady-in-waiting to Mary Queen of Scots. Then she married Sir James. No one quite knows why. She is beautiful, intelligent, caring and witty. Quite the opposite of her husband.

MARGARET "MEG" LUMLEY
Not a member of the family, but needs to be included for she seems to be involved in all of Will's tales. A poor peasant and serving girl, but bright, fearless and honest (she says). Also beautiful under her weather-stained skin and the most loyal friend any family could wish for (she says).

The Queen of the Dying Light

Chapter One

The Quest of the Dying Light

Chapter One

"Gone, forever gone"

Two men dug among the graveyard bones. In the dying light of the autumn evening they worked steadily at making a new grave. They threw aside the white bones of long-dead villagers. Then their shovels rang on something hard and black.

One man dropped lightly into the open grave and chipped a piece of the black rock loose. He picked it up, smelled it, and smiled a gap-toothed grin. "Gold," he breathed. "Black gold! Sir James Marsden will be pleased to see this!"

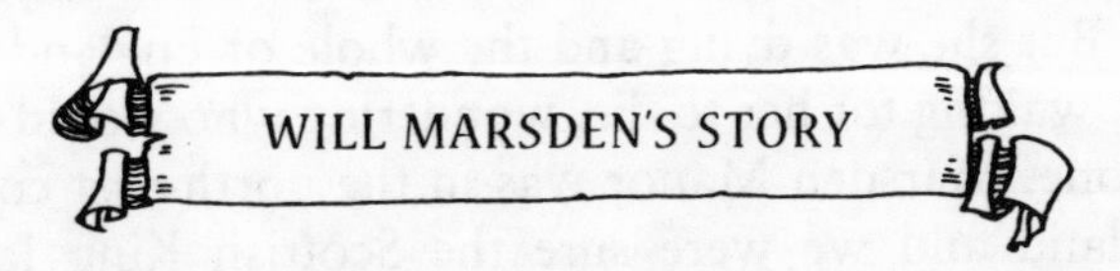

I remember. It was that time of year when everything had begun to die.

The days were growing shorter and evening shadows would race across the lawns in my home at Marsden Hall. The high stone walls held back winter cold for a while, but not for ever. The roses were withering and brown-edged petals blew over the grass and drifted against the solid oak doors.

As I walked towards the house from the stable yard a stranger came out. He had the cruellest face I have ever seen. It was as hard-edged as a chisel. His black eyebrows were straight, over narrow slits of eyes and a razor nose. His mouth was as tight as a rabbit trap. He was dressed in black from head to toe with only a small white shirt collar showing. He was replacing a wide-brimmed hat over dark hair that was cropped close to his flat skull.

"Good evening, sir," I said.

He looked through me as if I were a servant and not the heir to Marsden Manor, then brushed past me.

I closed the door against the cold and went in to dinner beside a large log fire in the great hall.

"Who was that man?" I asked my father.

He raised his chin with its pointed beard and looked down at me. "I don't know who you mean," he said. He said it in a voice that warned me not to ask. I sat down at the table with my parents and grandparents and Great-Uncle George.

Winter was always my favourite time when I was a boy at Marsden Hall. That was when we had supper around the table by the fire and then told stories.

Queen Elizabeth was on the throne in those days, of course. But she was dying and the whole of England was restless, waiting for her to die, wondering who would take her throne. Marsden Manor was in the north-east corner of England and we were sure the Scottish King James would march down and take the old Queen Elizabeth's throne. The Scots had always hated us. Some of James's Scottish subjects could well have been looking for more than having their king on the English throne. They could have been looking for revenge for old wounds and payment for old scores.

In a way we wanted the Queen to die so all the uncertainty would end. In another way we wanted her to live for ever so we'd never have to face our secret terrors.

"They say her mother was a witch," my grandmother

said suddenly. She was sitting closest to the fire. The thick white make-up on her ancient face reflected the flickering orange flames and her small dark eyes stared fifty years into the past.

"Who is that, Mother?" my father asked. "Who is a witch? Marsden Manor has never been troubled by witches." He was the magistrate for the district and he'd have remembered if he'd hanged a witch.

"Our good Queen Elizabeth. Her mother, Anne Boleyn, was a witch, they say."

"Hah!" Grandfather snorted. "It takes one to know one."

There had been a time when their bitter words had frightened me, but I was old enough now to know it was just their way of teasing. Grandmother looked up and gave a thin smile. "You met Anne Boleyn once, Clifford," she said to her husband. "She was a wicked, cruel, greedy little woman. But she wasn't a witch."

Great-Uncle George loosened his belt, lay back in his seat and stretched his legs towards the fire. His thick white beard made him look fierce, but he was as old as my grandparents and even his great strength was decaying. "She had six fingers on her left hand, you know," he said.

"If she was such a witch, how come she didn't turn herself into a falcon and fly through the window of her prison?" asked Grandmother. "Eh? Tell me that, George? She was a *woman*. It was a woman who knelt down for the headsman's sword."

"Don't you mean 'axe'?" my mother asked quietly. She had stayed at the table where the candles lit her tapestry work. Her maidservant, Meg, sorted the silk threads and practised her own small square of work.

"No, no, no!" Grandmother said, irritated. "You are thinking of Mary Queen of Scots. For Anne Boleyn's execution, they brought an expert swordsman across from France. She knelt on the straw and said her prayers. The executioner had hidden the sword under the straw. He asked someone to pass him the sword, and Queen Anne turned to look across the room at the person he'd spoken to. So she never saw him pick the sword out of the straw and sweep it down in a single movement. She died without the terror of waiting."

"That was kind of Henry," my grandfather sneered. He'd fought for the old king in the Scottish wars and learned to hate him.

"Henry was a fat and vicious boar of a man," Grandmother said. "He left Anne Boleyn's child without a mother. No wonder Princess Elizabeth grew up to be so strange."

"You're not saying the Queen's a witch, are you?" my grandfather asked.

Grandmother raised her shining black stick with the silver head and waved it at him. "No. But I am saying she *uses* witchcraft."

"You can't accuse the Queen of using witchcraft!" I gasped. "You could be executed for saying that!"

"You couldn't find an axe sharp enough to cut through her neck!" Grandfather chuckled.

Grandmother looked at him sourly. "It's a well-known fact. Elizabeth tried to murder her own sister with the help of a magician!"

I groaned and my father said angrily, "Really, Mother, you cannot go around saying that."

"I can if it's *true*," she replied. Then she sniffed. "Anyway, no one in this room is going to report me, are they?"

"Who was the magician?" Meg asked. Her sea-green eyes sparkled in the firelight, which turned her chestnut hair as red as one of the Queen's wigs. I had seen portraits of Elizabeth and her flaming hair was dazzling, but false.

Grandmother turned to Meg. "The magician was a weasel of a man called John Dee. He called himself *Doctor* Dee, although he had no right to do that. John Dee knew all about mathematics and astronomy. He was a greedy little man and he wanted to use his knowledge to make himself rich."

"You met him?" I asked.

"Met him?" she said, and gave a chuckle that made her cough and gasp for breath. She pressed a hand against her thin neck and struggled to get her breath. She wiped her watering eyes and said quietly to me, "Met him, Will? I saved his life!"

And I knew we were in for a story. I could see the family relax and settle back. It was Grandmother's turn to entertain and instruct us …

Fat old Henry VIII died. His body was rotting, and he had great sores on his legs that oozed through the bandages and the white stockings and gave him terrible pain. It was no more than the monster deserved. In the end they had to use a winch to hoist him up the stairs to his bed.

I'd served his second wife, Anne Boleyn – till he had her beheaded. Then I returned to serve his fifth wife, Katherine Howard. Poor little Katherine. She was a child. Just nineteen years old, married to that bloated ox of a man who smelled like the drains beneath Hampton Court Palace.

The child Katherine was bored – who can blame her? And she was full of life. It was no wonder that she flirted with handsome young men in the palace. We all knew she'd be caught one day and suffer Henry's vengeance. I married Sir Clifford Marsden and escaped before that happened. I didn't want to see another young queen die.

And, sure enough, in time Henry found out and sentenced her to die. They say Katherine ran through Hampton Court screaming to beg the King for mercy. He had the door barred, and she sobbed and beat her hands against it till her fingers bled. He must have heard her, but he ignored the child and sent her to her death. They say her howling spirit haunts the palace to this day.

So don't ask me to be sorry for that monstrous man. He died in agony and I hope he's down in Hell right now.

King Henry left three children, as you know. The sickly Edward, the half-mad Mary and the neglected Elizabeth. Edward didn't last long. He died of some dreadful disease.

The crown passed to his sister Mary and she brought terror to our country. She sliced the head off little Jane Grey because the girl dared to make a claim to the throne. The child was only sixteen. She was forced to watch her husband go to the block and then see his headless body brought back. Then she followed. Mary was as ruthless as her father.

Even in a distant corner like Marsden Manor we were afraid of Mary. Henry and his son Edward had made us all Protestants. Mary wanted to make us all Catholics again. A lot of people died horribly, burned at the stake, for trying to keep their Protestant faith.

Here in Marsden we went to whatever church our rulers told us. All we wanted was a quiet life. Imagine my terror when a troop of soldiers arrived at the gate, wearing the Tudor rose on their uniforms. I was in the garden, tending the herbs, when they clattered in, churning up the turf beneath their hooves.

"Sir Clifford Marsden?" their sergeant asked.

"Who wants to know?" I demanded. I should have lowered myself in a curtsey and showed them some respect. But that's never been my way. I've served queens and I wasn't going to grovel to a bunch of bully boys.

"I come from Queen Mary," the sergeant said.

I wondered what my husband had done to deserve her attention. I felt sick with fear at what they'd do to him. I

didn't want to watch him burn. "He's served her loyally," I said. "He's on the Border now, protecting her subjects from the Scottish cattle thieves."

The sergeant looked annoyed. "So who is in charge of the manor while he's away?" he demanded.

"I am," I told him.

He looked down at me with some disgust, but dismounted to stand beside me. He pulled a packet from his saddle-bag. It was sealed with Mary's great wax seal. "I suppose you had better read this," he said. "You *can* read, can you?"

"Not as well as a man," I said, with my sweetest smile. "But well enough."

He passed the packet across to me. I couldn't wait to open it, so I quickly arranged to have cheese and ale served to the soldiers in the kitchen while I went into the gallery. Our steward served the sergeant with wine and white bread while I took a seat by the window. The portraits of all the Marsden ancestors gazed down from the walls as I broke the seal and opened the packet.

The message to my husband was quite short. It made my heart stop beating for a minute, I'll swear. It ordered him to send his wife – me – to Queen Mary. If he disobeyed he was a traitor who would die a traitor's death. My hand was trembling as I finished reading. The sergeant was looking at me with a smug grin.

"I am ordered to present myself to Queen Mary," I said.

"And I am ordered to escort you to London," he said. "We can leave this afternoon."

"The estate!" I said. "My husband. What about them?"

"Leave your steward in charge of the estate and send messages to your husband. Be ready to leave in an hour."

Of course it took much longer to pack my best gowns, change into my riding clothes, write notes to my husband and find a messenger who would carry them to Alnwick, Morpeth and Berwick in the hope that one would find him. We only got as far south as Durham that night, but every day we covered fifty miles. The best horses were waiting for us at the best inns. By the fifth afternoon we were riding into Hampton Court.

This was the palace where I'd served Henry's wives. It was like coming home, but Queen Mary made it feel more like coming into prison. She was sitting in her apartment and I knelt in front of her. She did not ask me to sit down. For a quarter of an hour I had to kneel on the carpet,

my head bowed, while she told me of her suffering. *Her* suffering! I had ridden for five days, my body was aching and I was hungry.

"My sister wants to take my life and my crown," she said. Queen Mary had the same plain, pale face as her mother, Catherine of Aragon. Her eyes bulged unpleasantly and she began to pace the floor restlessly.

"I'm sure your sister loves you," I said quietly. It was a dangerous thing to say, but I had to take risks if I was going to survive this interview.

"My sister has plotted to kill me," she said.

"If Your Majesty says so," I nodded.

"Not everyone in England is loyal to me. They hate my husband Philip because he is Catholic."

"The people are more worried because he is *Spanish*," I said.

The Queen turned furiously. "It is no business of the people who I marry!"

"No, Your Majesty."

"Thomas Wyatt led a rebellion against me," she said.

"And he was caught and executed," I said. Even in Marsden Manor we knew the details of the plot.

"He wanted Elizabeth on the throne. *My* throne!"

"But Elizabeth wasn't part of that plot," I said.

"So she *says*. I locked her in the Tower of London – the Tower where her evil mother lost her wicked little head. But she wouldn't confess."

"I'm sure she was innocent," I said calmly.

"I have not been able to prove a thing," Mary cried. "But the plots go on. Now I've scotched a plan by Henry Dudley and John Throckmorton. All these plots to put Elizabeth on the throne!"

"They are not her fault," I said. I shifted slightly to ease the ache in my knees.

Mary came closer to me and bent her head near to mine.

I had not seen her since my days in Henry's court, but I had heard that she suffered some disgusting disease. As she leaned forward, the stench from her nostrils was sickening. I nearly vomited on her fine carpet. I tried to hold my breath and steady my heaving stomach.

"Elizabeth is behind these plots," Mary went on. "She is twisted. She is just like her mother – cunning and greedy for power. But I am going to put a stop to her plan. I am going to plant a spy in her household. I am going to find out exactly what she is planning, then bring young Elizabeth to trial."

"If she is guilty, she will deserve it," I said carefully.

"She *is* guilty. She *will* deserve it," said Mary, and her eyes flashed dangerously. "My spy will prove it."

"Only if Elizabeth trusts the man," I said.

"My spy will not be a man, it will be a woman."

"Then Elizabeth must trust this woman."

"She will," Mary said. She had a smirk on her thin lips. "My spy served Elizabeth's mother Anne Boleyn."

"Then I must know her!" I said.

Mary drew back her head and looked down her nose at me. "Mistress Eleanor, why do you think I have called you all the way from your pathetic little estate at the other end of the earth?"

"I – I don't know, Your Majesty."

"It is because I want *you* to serve Princess Elizabeth the way you served her vixen mother. The spy in Elizabeth's palace will be *you*, Eleanor."

Chapter Two

"My heart is heavy and mine age is weak"

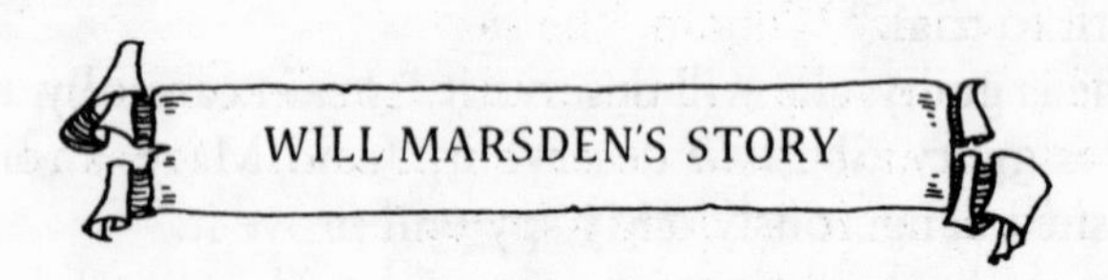

My grandmother coughed. The sound was like a dry stick dragged against a stone wall.

"You were a spy against Queen Elizabeth?" I asked.

"Will!" my mother said sharply. "This is no time for a story. Your grandmother's unwell." She put down her tapestry and rose to her feet. "Help me get Lady Eleanor to bed, Meg," she said.

Meg jumped to obey and gave me a glare to show that she too disapproved of me. "Can I do anything to help?" I asked.

"Catch some spiders," Grandfather said, with a harsh chuckle. "I knew a village wise man who said that the best cure for a cough was to swallow a live spider smothered in butter."

"Did it work?" I asked with a shudder.

"Work! I'll say it did! If someone threatened to push a greasy spider into your mouth, you'd stop coughing soon enough!"

Meg and my mother helped Grandmother to her feet and almost carried her out of the room. She dropped her cane and left it where it lay in the hearth. My father cleared his throat. He didn't like sickness in the house. "It's the autumn mist. Cools the blood too much and brings on the ague."

"She spends too much time in that garden," Great-Uncle George grumbled. "At her age she should take more care of herself."

There was a rapping on the front door and we turned as the steward came into the room. He stood in front of my father and gave a respectful bow of the head. "There is a message for Master William," he said.

My father took it from him, took a small coin from the purse at his belt and handed it to the steward. "It has come from Stratford, sir. It is a long journey."

My father looked sour and found another coin for the messenger. "Give him that," he ordered. He turned the packet over in his hand. "This will be from our friend Master William Shakespeare," he said.

"It's addressed to me, Father."

"I wonder what it's about. Probably wants my advice on a legal matter." My father had considered actors to be no better than vagrants and vagabonds until he met Master Shakespeare earlier that year. The playwright was a gentleman with his own coat of arms. More importantly, to my father, he was a wealthy and successful man of business.

"I think Master Shakespeare may be sending me news of the theatres," I tried to explain. "They were closed all summer because of the plague in London. He promised to let me know when they opened again."

"You'll be off to London to join his players," my father sighed. "I had hoped you would stay at Marsden and manage the estate."

I clenched my hands tightly and managed to keep my voice calm. "When I am older, Father," I said. We'd talked about this many times before.

He looked at the packet sadly and handed it to me. Grandfather and Great-Uncle George turned enquiringly towards me. I could see that I would get no privacy to read my letter.

"What does Master Shakespeare say?" Grandfather demanded.

"He sends you all his best wishes and hopes you are in good health," I mumbled as I read quickly. "And the playhouses open again in two weeks" time ... and our company has been chosen to perform for the Queen at Richmond Palace for the Christmas celebrations!"

"If she lives that long," Grandfather snorted.

"What will you perform?" Great-Uncle George asked. "Not that *Richard II* about a dying king. The Queen would hate that!"

"No. A new play Master Shakespeare has written specially," I said. "It's called *All's Well that Ends Well.* He's sent me a copy of my part."

I wanted nothing more than to hurry to my room and read the new play, but Grandfather delayed me. "When do you leave for London?"

"On the next coal ship from Wearmouth," I said. "When is that, Father?"

"The *Hawk* is loading now. She'll leave on tomorrow afternoon's high tide."

"Would you do one thing for me before you go?" Grandfather asked.

"Of course."

"Go and see old Jane Atkinson in her cottage in Bournmoor Woods. She may have some cure to soothe your grandmother's cough."

I smiled. It would be good to see the old wise woman again before I left. Unkind people called her a witch, but she was just very clever in the ways of nature. And she knew a lot about people. "I'll go at sunrise," I promised.

"Where?" Meg asked, as she walked back into the room.

"To see Jane Atkinson for a cure for Grandmother."

Meg nodded. "If anyone can cure her, Jane can. Perhaps Sir James can pay her!" she added brightly, looking towards my father.

"Pay her! For boiling up a few garden weeds?" he said, choking at the thought of having to open his purse again.

"No. Pay her for her lifetime of wisdom," Meg said. "Your mother's life must be worth a small fortune in gold."

"Of course! Of course!" my father said and handed her two groats.

I hardly slept that night. There was the excitement of reading the play and then a tap at the door around midnight. "Come in, Meg," I sighed.

"Is it good?"

"What?"

"The play?"

"Marvellous. Master Shakespeare's plays are always wonderful."

"Tell me what it's about."

"Meg! I want to sleep! I have to pack and get to Wearmouth tomorrow. I'll need to be up early."

"Me too. I'm coming to London with you."

"I thought you might be."

"Well, try to look pleased," she grinned.

"I am overcome with joy," I said. "Go away."

"And we have to see Jane Atkinson first, remember."

"I remember. Now go away."

She jumped to her feet. Only an owl should be so lively at that time of night. "I'll wake you at dawn," she promised brightly, as she slipped out of the room.

I groaned. My eyes hurt with the effort of reading by candle-light. I snuffed the candles and lay back on my bed, but I couldn't sleep. Tomorrow I was going to join Master Shakespeare's acting company at the Globe Theatre.

Within three months I'd be performing for the Queen herself. It was too exciting to sleep.

Almost as soon as I finally dozed off, I was woken by Meg shaking my shoulder. I dressed in a daze and splashed cold water on my face from a bowl at my bedside. The servants were stirring and I knew they'd have breakfast ready by the time I returned. Of course I thought I would be half an hour at the most.

We stepped out into the damp morning. The smoke from the fires was climbing straight into the dull grey sky. The tops of the trees vanished into a fine mist which muffled every sound. Even the sound of our footsteps died on the path. It was as if the silence were listening to silence.

For some reason it oppressed us, and we didn't talk as we left the high walls of Marsden Hall behind us and headed for Bournmoor Woods. When we reached the crossroads Meg finally spoke. "It's early for horsemen to be about," she said softly. "I wonder what they want."

I strained my ears. "I can't hear horses," I said.

She looked at me in a pitying way and said, "There are fresh hoof-prints on the ground. At least three horses went this way not long ago." She pointed to some prints on the Newcastle road. "You see yesterday's prints? They've crumbled at the edges and gone soft in the damp air. But these are fresh and sharp."

"Poachers in Bournmoor Woods?" I asked. I wished I'd had my sword with me.

"We haven't time to find out," Meg said.

We followed the tracks into the shadows of the wood. It was gloomier than ever. Even the crows were silent that morning. The only sound was the patter of water as the mist gathered on the bare branches and dropped on to the dead leaves below. But there were figures darker than any crows moving around the cottage in the clearing. Three men in black suits and hats were dragging the tall, frail figure of Widow Atkinson from her cottage. They pulled her roughly into her garden where she stumbled and fell

The old woman's hair was loose – she had not had time to finish dressing and put on her cap. Meg gave a cry of fury and rushed towards the men. They turned to see who was screaming at them and I recognized one of the men. The man with the chisel face. A white face with straight black eyebrows and no expression on the bloodless lips. I drew my knife and ran after Meg.

Her heavy velvet dress slowed her down, and I caught her before she reached the men and hauled her back by the arm. I jumped in front of her and snatched at the black jerkin of the man with the hard face. I brought my dagger up to within an inch of his throat. His narrow eyes glared at me with contempt, but no fear. "You villain!" I roared. "I arrest you in the name of Sir James Marsden."

I heard a soft swish as the two henchmen drew their daggers and I heard Meg cry, "Look out, Will!"

I pulled at my prisoner and swung him round so he stood between me and the fat red-faced man on one side. Then I turned to watch what the thinner and younger one was doing. His eyes showed his fear as he held his dagger at arm's-length and stepped carefully towards me. Suddenly a stone smacked the side of the man's hat and it toppled to the ground, uncovering his badly-cropped head.

The young man turned uncertainly towards Meg and waved a dagger at her. She already had another stone in her hand. "The next one won't knock your hat off, it'll knock your head off. Drop your dagger," she ordered, "or I'll spill your brains over the grass."

He lowered the knife and looked at her. Meg held the stone, poised to throw it. The fat man looked at the hard-faced man for orders and I held my dagger to his throat. Everyone in the garden was as still as the morning air.

Then the stranger spoke. I could feel my knife tremble as I rested it on his throat. "We are on Her Majesty the Queen's lawful business."

He had an accent that was almost Scottish. I'd heard it before when I'd been on the Borders in Northumberland. Meg reacted first. "The Queen allows you to attack harmless old women now, does she?"

The man turned his eyes towards her. It wasn't easy with my knife at his throat. "The Queen allows us to seek out and destroy witches," he said.

"Jane Atkinson's no witch!" Meg replied furiously.

"In that case she will be found not guilty and set free."

"You pulled her out of her cottage!" Meg cried and hurried over to the old woman. "I saw you. You've already decided she's guilty."

"We have a duty to search her home. She tried to stop us. We are allowed to use force." He strained forward till I was sure he would cut his own throat on my knife. "The Devil will be happy to use force. If the Devil is in her, he will destroy us before we enter the cottage."

Meg took a handkerchief from her pocket and soaked up dew from the grass to wipe her friend's brow. The old woman's eyes opened. She looked more sad than hurt or frightened. "She's innocent!" Meg cried.

The man began to breathe more quickly. "None of us is *innocent*!" he said. "We are all sinners! *You* as well as the rest. And you will hang too if you stand in our way." Suddenly he fastened a thin white hand round my wrist and pulled my dagger away from his throat. "I am here on the authority of the magistrate of Marsden Manor."

"My father's the magistrate," I said, tearing my hand free from his iron grip.

"A good, honest man who will be happy to see his son hang if I order it."

"If *you* order it!" I gasped. "Who are you?"

"I am Calvin Cartwright and you will do well to remember that name, boy. This is my brother, Luther Ramsbottom," he said pointing at the red-faced man. "And this is my brother, Knox Brodie," he added, waving a hand towards the young thin man.

"If they're your brother, why aren't you all called Cartwright?" asked Meg.

"We are brothers in the sight of God. We will now search the cottage and we will deal with you later," he said, turning on his heel and stooping to enter the low doorway.

"Puritans," said Widow Atkinson. She was pale and shaking a little, but she was able to sit up. "Worse than Catholics. They give the Queen just as much trouble too."

There was the sound of breaking pottery from inside the cottage. I moved to see what they were doing, but Jane Atkinson stopped me. "There's nothing of value in there. I came into this world with nothing and I'll go out with nothing."

Luther appeared at the door, a piece of smouldering turf on the end of his knife blade. Slowly he raised the turf to the straw roof.

"No!" Meg cried. "That's wicked!"

The straw caught fire and hissed and crackled as the yellow flames lapped hungrily at the roof. Calvin Cartwright and Knox Brodie hurried out. The leader strode over to the widow and said, "I arrest you in the Queen's name. The charge is witchcraft."

"She has to have a trial," I objected.

"She *shall* have a trial."

"You have no proof!" Meg cried.

He stretched out a long arm and showed her a clenched fist. "Witches have familiars. Creatures sent by the Devil to help them. We have found Jane Atkinson's familiar," he said.

The fire flared behind him like the fire of Hell itself. Slowly he turned his fist over, uncoiled his long fingers and showed us what he held in his hand.

"The book of Exodus tells us, 'You shall not permit a witch to live'," he said. We looked at his hand and the warty toad on his palm stared back at us.

Chapter Three

"The devil it is that's thy master"

Luther Ramsbottom and Knox Brodie grabbed Widow Atkinson roughly by the arms. "Where are you taking her?" Meg demanded.

"To Magistrate Marsden," Calvin Cartwright said. "A witch must be brought to trial."

"She's a helpless old woman!" I said.

In Cartwright's cold eyes I saw a glimmer of joy. "Aye, helpless without her familiar to help her!"

Meg tore at the hands of the Puritans and said, "I'll help Mistress Atkinson to the magistrate's house." She placed one of the widow's arms around her shoulders and slowly set off for Marsden Hall. I ran ahead to warn my father. It was brighter now, but the sun wasn't warm enough to burn the mist away. Labourers were coming

out of their cottages to work in the fields, or so I thought.

At the crossroads I met the local horse thief, Wat Grey, and his greasy friend Michael the Taverner. They spent every night drinking in the Black Bull Tavern and usually rose in time for dinner. I couldn't remember seeing either of them at dawn.

"Where are you going?" I asked.

Michael Taverner looked at me through watery, red-rimmed eyes and said, "To Marsden Hall for the trial, of course. Everyone in the village will be there." Sweat and

the morning mist ran down his face and left white streaks in the dirt.

"What trial?" I asked.

"The witch trial," Wat Grey said, his grin showing dirty yellow teeth.

"Which trial?"

"Hah! You mean which witch trial, don't you?" Wat laughed at his feeble joke and Michael gave a rumbling chuckle.

"Who is being tried?" I said carefully.

"Old Jane Atkinson, of course."

I shook my head, bewildered. "But she was only arrested two minutes ago. How do you know about the trial?"

Michael Taverner waved a grubby hand at the stream of people coming from their cottages. "Everyone knows. The Puritans were outside the tavern last night asking for witnesses."

I realized that the labourers coming from their cottages weren't heading for the fields. They had their wives and children with them and they were making for Marsden Manor. They were as excited as if they were on their way to the Chester-le-Street fair. Some were even dressed in their best clothes.

"Witnesses to what?" I asked, as I hurried after the taverner.

"Witnesses to Jane Atkinson's witchcraft!" he told me.

"But she isn't a witch!"

"That's not the point, is it? The point is that the Puritans *suspect* her and Jane Atkinson has one or two enemies who want to see her hang."

I pushed through the crowd at the gate to Marsden Hall and ran into the house. My father, Grandfather and Great-Uncle George were putting on their magistrates" robes and the dining table was being moved to the window for them to sit behind.

"Ah, Will!" Grandfather said. "Just in time. Take your parchment and quill. We need you to make notes."

"What's going on?" I cried.

"We are going to have to try Jane Atkinson," he said. "These Puritan fellows have travelled down from the Borders. King James up there has a passion for seeking out witches on his side of the Border. These men are clearing out the English witches before he arrives to take the throne."

"The Queen isn't dead yet," I reminded him.

"Nobody lives for ever," he said with a sigh.

"Not even Grandmother," I said bitterly.

"What was that?"

"Jane Atkinson is the only person who can save Grandmother. If you sentence her to hang, you'll be sentencing your own wife to death."

He looked pained at the thought. "I know, my boy. I

know. But we have to show Scottish James that we are willing. Jane has no case to answer. We'll go through the trial and then let her go."

"Does my father know of your plan?" I asked.

"Of course, of course." He wrapped an arm around my shoulders and led me to the window. The villagers were streaming over the lawns and jostling to get into the house. They stopped and went quiet as Meg helped the widow through the main gates followed by the three men in black suits. "These are dangerous times, Will. If we want to survive we have to keep the Puritans happy. They say that James himself holds on to power in Scotland by helping them. Trust us, Will. Trust us."

I sat at the table and spread out my writing equipment while Jane Atkinson was led into the hall and the villagers crowded after her.

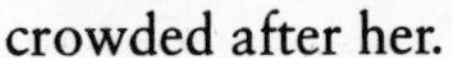

Meg insisted that the old woman should be allowed to sit down and she stood at her shoulder, glaring at me behind the table. I felt like a traitor and couldn't meet her fierce gaze.

My father took his seat at the table and said quickly, "I call this court to order. Who brings a charge?"

Calvin Cartwright stepped forward. He seemed to grow in height now that he had an audience. He looked around at the open-mouthed villagers before he spoke. "I do. I have evidence that this woman, Widow Jane Atkinson, did consort with the Devil to perform evil deeds."

"That's a serious charge," Great-Uncle George said. He and Grandfather had grown up with Jane Atkinson and they liked her. My great-uncle was having trouble controlling his temper and the air was like Widow Atkinson's cottage roof, just waiting for a spark that would set it alight.

Cartwright turned his gaze on Great-Uncle George. "Beware that this woman has not bewitched you too, Sir George. Those who stand up for a proven witch will hang alongside her."

"Do you dare to threaten me!" the old man exploded.

The Puritan stared at him and said quietly, "You know your duty, Sir George."

"I do. And I don't need some pompous, shaven-headed pilgarlic like you to remind me what it is."

The crowd gasped at his strong language and my father rested a hand on his uncle's arm to calm him. "Can we hear the evidence, Master Cartwright?"

The Puritan turned slowly towards the watching villagers and said, "Step forward, Adam Field."

A young carter with a face scarred by smallpox stepped forward and twisted his leather cap between his hands. He looked at the floor.

Cartwright asked him, "Will you tell the magistrates what you told me last night, Field?"

The young man began to mutter in a voice so low I could barely catch his words. "I went to Widow Atkinson with a toothache. She boiled a holly leaf, put it in a saucer of water, and told me to yawn over the saucer so the poisonous tooth-worms would fall out of the tooth."

A lot of people nodded at this. It was an old way of curing the toothache.

"And what did the witch do while she was boiling the holly leaf?" Cartwright asked.

"She asked me how my mother was," Adam Field said.

"Didn't she *also* mutter a spell over the boiling water?"

"Her lips were moving . . ." the carter began.

"Exactly!" Cartwright hissed. "What else could she have been doing, but praying to Satan her master?"

"She could have been praying to God!" Meg cut in.

Cartwright turned on her. "Quiet, child. We may need to deal with you after the witch." He looked at the crowd of people and asked, "Is Sarah White here?"

A milkmaid stepped forward. She walked with a limp and, like Adam Field, didn't dare look anyone in the face. "Sarah," Cartwright said, as gently as he could, "you went to Witch Atkinson last winter, didn't you?"

"Aye."

"Tell the magistrates why."

"My best cow weren't giving no milk."

"What did Witch Atkinson tell you?"

"Told me it was my fault for trying to milk the cow with cold hands."

"And that was all?"

"She wouldn't give me no cure."

"So you were upset?"

"I called her a few names."

"What names?"

Sarah blushed a deep pink and looked at the shoes of everyone in front of her. "Rude names."

"You called the witch rude names? And what happened to you?"

"Next time I went to milk the cow she kicked me. Broke my leg! The witch put a curse on me for calling her names!"

Meg leaned forward. "And *I'd* kick you if you tried to milk me with cold hands in winter!"

The villagers laughed, but the laughter died when the Puritan scowled at them. Widow Atkinson whispered something in Meg's ear and the girl nodded. "Sarah," Meg said. "You went back to Widow Atkinson in the summer, didn't you?"

"Maybe."

Cartwright stepped towards Meg. "You have no right to ask questions in this court!"

Meg looked at Grandfather. "May I speak for Jane Atkinson?" she said simply.

"Go ahead," Grandfather told her.

Meg gave Cartwright a tight smile and turned back to the milkmaid. "Why did you go back to Widow Atkinson? If you thought she was a witch, why go back to her?"

Sarah shrugged and said nothing.

Cartwright cut in. "Sarah, you went back to Widow Atkinson for a love potion, didn't you? You wanted a young man in the village to fall in love with you, didn't you?"

"Maybe," the milkmaid said sulkily.

"Shall I tell everyone the young man's name?"

"No! No!" Sarah cried and looked up for the first time.

"What did Widow Atkinson tell you?"

"She said there was an old spell. I had to scatter rose

petals on the path in front of the young man. If he stepped over them he'd fall in love with the next girl he saw."

Again the villagers nodded. They knew that old spell. "Did it work?"

"No!" Sarah said and her mouth turned down as if she'd swallowed a mouthful of her own sour milk. "He stepped over the rose petals all right," she said bitterly. "But Ginny Bell was the next girl he saw and he went off and married her!"

Now everyone in the room knew who the young man was and Sarah White's face was burning with shame and confusion. "That wasn't Widow Atkinson's fault!" Meg cried.

"Was!" Sarah snapped. "She cursed me. Broke my leg and then she sent cross-eyed Ginny Bell along the path ahead of me! She's a witch. That's what she is . . . a witch."

The villagers were muttering among themselves and having doubts now. Cartwright called over their voices, "And did you see a creature of the Devil when you visited her?"

"Yes!" Sarah said. "A butterfly in her garden!"

The villagers gasped. Butterflies were certainly one of the Devil's favourite disguises. "Any other of Satan's servants?" Cartwright went on.

"Yes! A hare! It was sitting by the fire!"

"Anything else?"

"A broomstick. She uses it to fly around the forest at night and meet other witches!" Sarah said. Her voice was breaking now with the excitement.

"Anything else? Any other creature?"

"A toad!" the girl cried.

Cartwright reached into his pocket and pulled out the creature he'd been holding at the burning cottage. "*This* toad?"

"That's the one! That's the one!" Sarah White screamed. "Take it away from me! That's Satan himself. He'll take all our souls."

The villagers were in uproar and some were pushing to get out through the hall door.

Cartwright slipped the toad back in his pocket and held up his palms to the girl. "You are safe here, Sarah. We are the blessed ministers of God. Satan cannot harm you while we are here to protect you."

Panting, she sank weakly to her knees. "Thank you, sir, oh, thank you." She buried her face in her hands and began to weep quietly.

Cartwright turned his back on the magistrates" table as if we didn't exist and spoke directly to the villagers. "You are sinners. All miserable sinners. But some of you will be saved and go to Heaven when you die. Some are the chosen ones. It is those chosen ones the Devil is after. If you have had dealings with this woman, then now is the time to confess and save your souls!"

For the next hour we had to listen to a stream of hatred and lies about Jane Atkinson. Each witness who stepped forward wanted to do better than the one before. Jane Atkinson cursed a child who died, Jane Atkinson caused a storm that ruined a field of wheat, Jane Atkinson used magic to find a chest of gold, Jane Atkinson danced with the Devil in the shape of a goat, and Jane Atkinson walked across the River Wear on her way to market.

Meg could no more stop the flow of lies than she could stop the rising tide in the North Sea. Jane Atkinson looked tired and empty. Meg looked defeated and shaken.

My father raised a hand and said, "Enough, Master Cartwright. We have heard enough."

The crowd fell silent and turned towards our table. Cartwright stood, his legs planted firmly astride and triumph in his narrow eyes. "You must find this woman guilty of witchcraft. The Bible says, 'You shall not permit a witch to live'."

"We know what the Bible says," Grandfather said. "But this is a court of English law. We follow Her Majesty Queen Elizabeth's witchcraft laws, not the Bible."

"And that English law says you must hang her!"

"You are mistaken there," my father said quietly. "The law says we must *examine* the accused woman. We need to hear her confess in her own words."

"And you can also use any form of torture you wish to *make* her confess," Cartwright said. He half-turned so that the watching villagers could hear him. "I was present when King James himself examined suspected witches. When the Pilniewinks were screwed on to a witch's thumbs till they bled; when an iron case called the Cashielaws was wrapped around the leg and slowly heated up; when the metal boot was strapped to a man's foot and wedges driven in till the leg was crushed; when the head-rope was knotted around the skull and tightened. King James watched it all."

"James is not *our* king," my father said quietly.

"Yet," Cartwright said even more quietly.

"Yet," my father agreed, with a small bow of his head. I didn't understand why my father was being so patient with this mad Puritan.

"Two of the Scottish witches confessed and were burned," Cartwright said. "In Scotland they burn witches because it makes the world so much purer."

"*You* would confess if you were tortured," Meg said.

Cartwright spread his long pale fingers wide. "Not true! One man was tortured till blood sprang from his crushed legs, and still he refused to confess."

"He was spared?" Great-Uncle George asked.

"No," Cartwright said. "King James said the Devil must have given him strength to face torture like that. The man was burned along with the rest."

"That's not fair!" Meg cried. "Burned if you confess and burned if you don't!"

"We do not need Scottish torture implements," Grandfather said angrily. "We have the old English witch-test . . . trial by water. The suspect is lowered into the water. If she sinks she is innocent, if she floats she's guilty."

"The ducking stool!" one of the villagers cried. "We haven't seen that for fifty years!"

"It'll be rotten by now," someone else sighed.

"Build a new one! Ellis the Carpenter can make us one."

"Silence!" Grandfather cried over the excited babble of voices. "The magistrates will examine Jane Atkinson." He turned to the widow. "There are a lot of charges to answer, Mistress Atkinson," he said gently. "You will be held under arrest in this house. We will ask you to explain the charges."

"You were always a fair man, Sir Clifford," Jane Atkinson said calmly.

"And this court is dismissed!" Great-Uncle George roared. "Get back to the fields before the winter storms drive you indoors."

The villagers grumbled, disappointed. Some had been cheated of their sport and others simply wanted to avoid the day's work.

Calvin Cartwright stayed where he was and his two henchmen lurked in the doorway.

"And you, Cartwright, can go witch-hunting somewhere else," said Great-Uncle George. "Perhaps you will be welcome in Scotland?"

Cartwright placed his wide-brimmed hat carefully on his cropped hair and said, "No, Sir George. I will be staying in this area for quite a while. I have bought some land and I'll be having a house built."

My heart sank at the thought of having this monstrous man in the county. "The Marsden family own all the land around here," Grandfather said. "You must have bought a plot of land from our neighbour, Lord Birtley."

"Oh, no, Sir Clifford. I bought the land from Sir James last night."

My father pretended to be busy with the papers on the table while Grandfather, Great-Uncle George and I stared at him. "Where is this land?" Grandfather asked.

"In the north-eastern corner of Bournmoor Woods," he said.

"Widow Atkinson's cottage is on that land," I said.

Calvin Cartwright almost smiled. He turned and walked towards the door where his two "brothers" were grinning. "Not any more," he said. "Not any more."

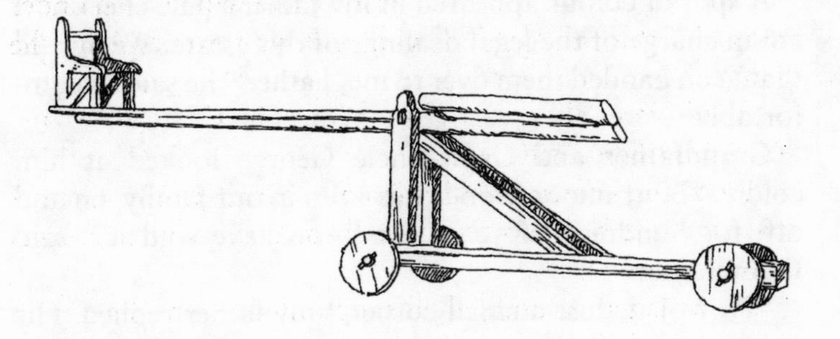

Chapter Four

"Who cannot be crushed with a plot?"

My father kept his head low and headed for the doorway to the hall. "Are we going to catch the ship for London?" I asked.

He stopped and turned on me furiously. "There is little point, William. Ships are not powered by coal and never will be. They are powered by the wind. And you may have noticed that there is no wind. We cannot sail until the weather changes."

He turned on his heel, but was halted by Grandfather who said quietly, "James. A word."

Father turned back. "So much to do ..." he fussed.

"Tell George and me about this deal you have done with the Puritan Cartwright."

A spot of colour appeared in my father's pale cheeks. "I am in charge of the legal dealings of this estate. We agreed that. You handed them over to me, Father," he said uncomfortably.

Grandfather and Great-Uncle George looked at him coldly. "Bournmoor Woods has been in our family, on and off, for hundreds of years. And you have sold it," said Grandfather.

"*Part* of it. Just a small corner," my father replied. His voice was a whine.

"Widow Atkinson's part of it," said Great-Uncle

George, looking towards the old woman who sat patiently watching.

"We can find her a cottage in the village," said my father.

"No, we can offer her a place in Marsden Hall," Grandfather told him sharply. "Your mother needs someone to care for her." He turned to the old woman. "Would you like to move in here?"

"I'd rather live in my own cottage," sighed Jane Atkinson. "But you are very kind. I will take your offer of shelter till I can go back home."

Grandfather nodded. "Now, James. What is this all about?"

My father shrugged himself deep into the fur collar of his robe and said, "Money. A fortune."

"You sold that corner of the woods for a fortune?"

"No, I exchanged it for richer land," he said, trying to smile.

"Where?"

"The Puritans own Marsden Church and the land around it."

"The graveyard?"

"The graveyard."

Grandfather pinched the top of his nose tiredly. "You exchanged the finest hunting park in Durham for a field full of bones?"

"Yes ... I mean, no! I exchanged it for our future fortune!"

"Explain," Great-Uncle George said gruffly.

"London is desperate for fuel. The people have burned every forest for fifty miles around and now they need coal to warm themselves in the winter. The price of coal is rising every year. We can sell as much as we can ship down there. And I have discovered that the churchyard is built on the thickest seam of the best Durham coal you've ever seen! It will make us a fortune!"

Meg stood behind Jane Atkinson and sighed. "And, when that coal is gone, you will be left with a waste heap of soil and stone. Bournmoor Woods would have lasted for ever."

"Everything changes," my father said. "We'll be rich!"

"But your grandchildren will be poorer without Bournmoor Woods," said Jane Atkinson.

"Why would you worry? You'll be dead!" my father raged, and he stalked out of the room.

He left behind a gloom as deep and silent as the morning mist in Bournmoor Woods. At last my grandfather spoke. "Sometimes I'm ashamed of my son," he said.

"Would you come and look at Lady Eleanor?" he said to Jane Atkinson. "She had a restless night. She couldn't sleep for coughing."

"I'll do what I can, Sir Clifford," said the widow, smiling bravely. "Of course a lot of my herbs will have been lost when they burned down my cottage."

"We have some herbs in the kitchen garden," Meg said helpfully.

Jane Atkinson rose stiffly. "Don't you want to duck me in the river first, Sir Clifford?" she asked.

Grandfather laughed. "Let's wait for winter when there's a good coating of ice, shall we? That'll teach you to upset the Puritans!"

"It isn't funny," Meg said.

Jane Atkinson groaned. "No, it's sad. That poor Adam Field and sad Sarah White."

"Poor and sad? They tried to have you hanged!" said Meg, her green eyes glowing with anger.

"They are unhappy. Unhappy people often have to find someone else to blame," she smiled. "Now let's go and look at Lady Eleanor, shall we?"

Meg led the way up the oak stairway and Jane Atkinson hobbled after her. Grandmother was in her bed with the curtains around it open and the weak morning light creeping through. My mother was feeding her some milky gruel. Grandmother had not put on her thick white make-up and her skin was cracked and dry. "Good morning, Jane," she said and coughed. She gasped for air, then said, "Come to kill me off with your cures, have you? Well, I'd rather die than swallow a spider in butter, I can tell you now!"

Grandfather and Great-Uncle George, Meg and I sat around the bed while Widow Atkinson placed a hand on Grandmother's forehead. "You have a slight fever, Lady

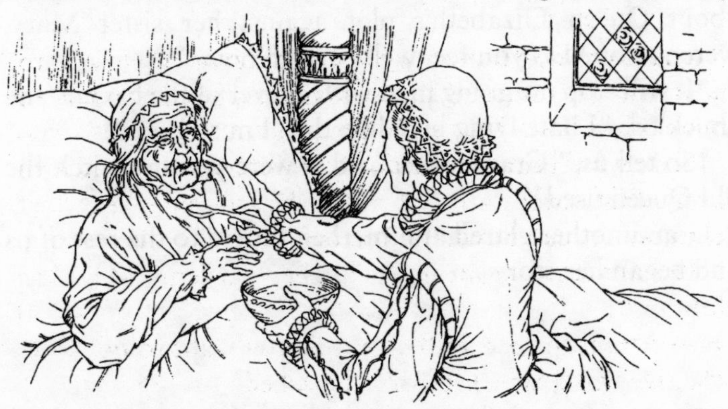

Eleanor. We'll deal with that first and then with the cough."

She sent Meg to the garden to gather herbs and to the kitchen for honey and warm wine. Great-Uncle George said, "Too much blood, Eleanor, that's your trouble. Want me to bleed you?" he asked and drew his knife.

"No!" Widow Atkinson said sharply. "If God had wanted to let out blood every time we're ill, he'd have fitted a tap to our arm! Just put that knife away. And leave your stepsister in peace."

Great-Uncle George shook his head and muttered that doctors *always* liked to let blood out of a sick person. "Just as well you have me to look after you," Jane Atkinson said, "or they'd be making black puddings from your blood, given half a chance."

"You're staying a while then?" Grandmother asked.

"Sir Clifford kindly offered me a roof over my head since my own has been burned down." And she told Grandmother of what had happened that morning.

"Wicked!" Grandmother cried.

"And unfair," my mother said. "Queen Elizabeth herself can use witchcraft. But when one of her subjects tries they get hanged!"

"Yes, Grandmother," I said. "You were going to tell us about Queen Elizabeth's plot against her sister Mary, weren't you? Do you feel well enough now?"

"It will stop me going mad with a fever of the brain," she chuckled. "I hate lying here like this. I'm so bored!"

"So tell us," Grandfather said. "Were *you* the witch the old Queen used?"

Grandmother glared at him, then turned to the rest of us and began her story …

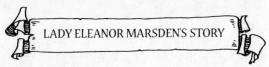

Elizabeth and Mary were as different as their mothers had been ... and they hated one another about as much. Mary had too much air and water in her spirit – Elizabeth had too much earth and fire. Far too much fire.

Queen Mary had asked me to spy on Princess Elizabeth and I had no choice. If I had refused, she could have sent her officers to look at the way we worshipped here in Marsden Hall. If Marsden Hall didn't burn, *I* would. So, I agreed.

Elizabeth was just twenty-five years old at the time and the most beautiful princess in the world. Her hair was as fiery as her spirit and her eyes as dark as winter pools. Those eyes looked clear through you. She had her father's temper and her mother's slyness. While she told Mary she was a loyal sister, she was waiting and plotting for her chance. I was too honest for my spying job.

I met her at Hatfield Palace and didn't dare look in those fierce eyes. "Lady Eleanor Marsden!" she said sweetly. "You've been sent by my sister Mary to spy on me."

I thought I was going to faint. "I am Your Grace's loyal and humble servant," I muttered, as I made a low curtsey. "I served your mother."

Princess Elizabeth took my hand and lifted me up. She was slightly shorter than me and looked annoyed that she had to look up at me. "Sit down," she said, waving to a seat in the window. She sat beside me. Even as a princess she had a taste for jewelled gowns, and the rubies dazzled me as we sat in the sunlight. Princess Elizabeth looked at me. "You have been sent to spy on me."

"I served your ..."

"Yes, yes. You served my mother, I know. But you are avoiding my question. Stepsister Mary sent you to report on me, didn't she?"

"Yes, Your Grace."

She nodded. "And so you shall!"

"I shall?"

"Of course. You will tell her exactly what I want you to tell her. That I am living happily here with my books and my music. That my only visitors are honest subjects of the Queen and I am forever telling them how much I love dear Mary." She sighed. "I only wish you were a better liar, Eleanor!"

"Then you *are* plotting against your sister."

"Stepsister," she reminded me. "England needs a powerful queen and Mary is not the woman to rule. She has an unpopular Spanish husband who has gone back to his filthy country and deserted her. She has gone to war with France and lost the land my father fought for so hard. She has burned our Protestant friends till we are choking on the smoke." She smiled suddenly. Her smile was as dazzling as her rubies when she wanted it to be. "Perhaps I don't need to plot against my stepsister," she said, and I saw her mother's slyness in her eyes.

"You think the people will rise against her anyway?" I asked. It was true there were murmurs of rebellion in Durham before I left.

The door to the princess's room opened and a lady-in-waiting said, "Doctor Dee is waiting now, Your Grace."

Princess Elizabeth held up a hand to keep her waiting a moment. "Lady Eleanor," she said quietly, "you have been sent here to spy on me. So I trust you. Mary thinks you will be loyal to her because she is your queen. But I know you will be loyal to *me* because I am *going to be* your queen!"

I didn't know how she could be so sure, but she waved a hand to allow her visitor into the room. "Let us meet the mystical Doctor Dee, shall we?" the princess asked.

The man who came into the room entered as if he were a priest coming into church. He was about thirty years old, but his long, serious face made him look much older. He was dressed in dusty black robes and a close-fitting black skullcap was pulled over his colourless hair. He looked at me from under thick eyebrows, his eyes dark and liquid.

"Doctor Dee, this is Mary's latest spy, Lady Eleanor Marsden from Durham. She's here to report your wicked plans to poison the Queen."

The man's small mouth went tight. "It is not a game, Your Grace. If Mary once suspects you are plotting against her, she will lock you in the Tower again."

Princess Elizabeth shrugged. "She wouldn't dare. I am much too popular."

"As you wish," he said with a bow. "But it is true you will not return to London as a prisoner, but as Queen."

The princess sprang to her feet with the grace of a cat and clasped her hands in front of her. "You have looked into your magic glass, Dee! What have you seen?"

The man's face was pained. "Your Grace, I beg you not to use the word *magic*. I am a mathematician and an astrologer."

"Yes, yes, Dee. You read the stars and you calculate the future. I don't care how you do it. Just tell me what you see!"

He unrolled a scroll of parchment and laid it on the table by the window. I had seen star charts like this before. These were carefully drawn and there were calculations scrawled in the margins. "The good news, Your Grace, is that you will live a long life and you will become Queen of England."

"But *when*, Dee, when?"

"That is the bad news. Sadly, your dear sister ..."

"Half-sister!" the princess said.

"As you say, your *half*-sister will not survive the year."

"Dee! Your are a true magician!" she cried and clapped her hands.

"Your Grace, I am *not* a magician!"

"Very well, you are just a *very* clever man. Now all I have to do is make sure the horoscopes come true. Have you the manikin, Dee?"

The man sighed and raised his eyes to the fine carved and painted ceiling. "Yes, Your Grace."

"Then give it to me," Princess Elizabeth demanded.

He reached into his robe and pulled out a wax figure about the length of his hand. It was crudely shaped into the form of a woman. "Do you know who this is, Lady Eleanor?"

"Your sister – I mean half-sister, Your Grace."

The princess nodded and took a long pin from the sleeve of her dress. "Doctor Dee is *not* a magician, of course," she said, smiling at him. "But he does have books about magic."

"I have a vast library on every subject," said Doctor Dee.

The princess bowed her head. "In his *vast* library he has many books on magic and witchcraft . . . although he is *not* a magician or a witch. And he has shown me some very strange practices. One needs a wax model of one's enemy . . . see? I have Mary here. Now, if the wax model has a wick through the middle, I set light to it and it burns like a candle. As the candle melts, so the enemy's life will melt away."

"I have heard that, Your Grace," I said.

"And the other way of harming the enemy is by sticking pins into the wax model. If I stick pins in the legs, Mary will suffer pains in her legs. If I place one in her heart, then she will die. Do you understand, Eleanor?"

"Yes, Your Grace," I said. I wondered why she was telling me this.

"Doctor Dee says this is nonsense, don't you, Dee?" The man remained silent. Princess Elizabeth repeated the question. "Don't you, Dee?"

"It has not been proved," he said.

The princess smiled. "Now is your chance to prove it, Dee. Stick a pin in the wax doll's heart."

Doctor Dee turned grey. "I . . . I cannot do that. It would be murder."

"But you don't believe it, Dee. You don't think it will do any harm, so *do* it!"

"I beg to be excused, Your Grace," he said.

Elizabeth turned to me. "But I *do* believe it will work. So I can't do it. I can't murder my own half-sister, can I?"

"No," I said shortly. At last I saw where this was leading.

"I think it would be right if Mary's own spy did this thing, don't you, Lady Eleanor?"

"Me?"

"Who else?"

My mouth was dry. If Dee was right and Elizabeth was soon to be our queen, a pin in a lump of shaped wax would make no difference. It was all in the stars. Elizabeth's small dark eyes were burning into me. I could feel the strength of her spirit forcing me to take the pin

from her. I held the pin in my right hand and the wax in my left. "God forgive me," I murmured, and I plunged the pin into the heart of the wax doll.

I was sweating and shivering at the same time. I think I expected the doll to scream. But nothing happened. The princess nodded gently. "You are a true and loyal subject, Eleanor. You too, Dee. You will be rewarded when I become Queen. Now go back to Mary and tell her all you have seen."

"All?" I asked. I knew that I would be executed for witchcraft if I confessed what I had done.

"Or as much as you wish," she said with her cat-clever smile. "After all, you *are* Mary's spy. She will expect a report."

A month later I stood in front of Queen Mary. The

stench from her nostrils sickened me. Her body was swollen with dropsy and her face showed the pain.

"I hope Your Majesty is well," I said.

"Last night they got into my bedroom," she hissed.

"Who, Your Majesty?"

"My enemies. They left a dead dog on the floor. They had cropped its ears and shaved its head. It was meant to be a message for my shaven-headed Catholic priests. A warning! But they won't frighten me. They won't stop me burning the unbelievers."

"No, Your Majesty," I said.

"So, what is Elizabeth doing with that magician Dee?" she asked.

"He reads horoscopes for her," I said.

"And what does he see?"

"He sees a long life for Elizabeth," I said carefully.

"Does he use magic to make me ill?" she asked.

"No, Your Majesty," I lied.

The Queen rolled her great pale eyes. "Someone does. Someone does. But it is good to know it is not my sister. I feel I have not long to live. I was going to name my husband Philip as my successor. But if what you say is true, Lady Eleanor, then I will name dear Elizabeth."

Within a month the bells in every church in the country were sounding their deafening message. They weren't ringing the slow toll of misery for the death of poor Mary. They were ringing peals of happiness for the new Queen. Queen Elizabeth.

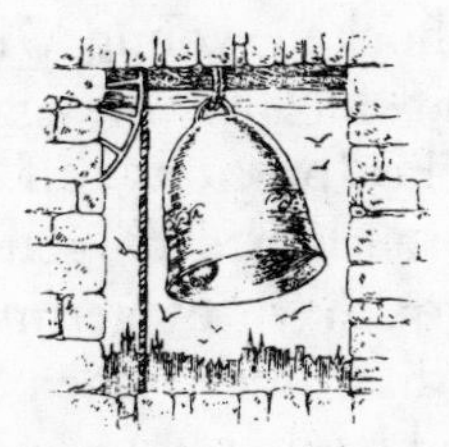

CHAPTER FIVE

"While shameful hate sleeps out the afternoon"

"You can't kill a person by sticking pins in a doll," Meg said.

Jane Atkinson nodded. "You're right, Meg, you can't. But there are a lot of people who *believe* you can. Queen Elizabeth believed it."

"And Queen Elizabeth believed I'd killed her sister," Grandmother said. "She promised me rich rewards if Mary died. She promised John Dee the same."

"What did she give you?" I asked.

Grandmother laughed softly, although it seemed to hurt her. "She gave me what she gave most people. Nothing. Nothing at all."

"She broke her promise?" I asked.

"Don't look so shocked, young Will. Our good Queen Elizabeth has spent all her life gathering riches and spending them on her precious self. She's grasping and greedy. You've more chance of getting a lamb from a wolf's jaws than you have of getting a groat from her purse. Remember that, Will, when you go to perform for her. She inherited her temper and her cruelty from her father, King Henry VIII. But she got her meanness from her grandfather, Henry VII."

"Henry VII returned Bournmoor Woods to the Marsdens," I said, remembering one of Great-Uncle George's stories.

"And now your father's started giving it away," said Grandmother. She lay back and closed her eyes wearily. It was time to let her rest again and we left the room quietly. Widow Atkinson stayed to give Grandmother the herb and honey mixture.

We gathered downstairs in the hall by the great stone fireplace and Mother arranged for us to have the breakfast that had been delayed for so long. When we'd eaten in gloomy silence Grandfather turned to me and said, "You will inherit the Marsden lands when your father and I have died. Do you want to go and look at your new property?"

"A graveyard?" I asked.

"Or a rich coalfield, if your father's to be believed," Meg said.

Of course Meg had to come with us. We wrapped well in woollen cloaks and walked through the walled garden

of the old house. We walked slowly because Grandfather was stiff. We passed the archway covered by climbing roses. They were shrivelling and falling now. Grandfather pointed to them. "The old roses have to die and fall. That's so the new, fresh ones can break through. The old must die so the new can thrive."

"Like Queen Elizabeth?" said Meg.

"That's right. It's time for her to go so we can have a real leader again. She's too tired and feeble. The whole country is rotting like those rose petals on the ground. The time of the Tudors is gone, and it's time for the Queen to let go."

When we reached the gateway on to the church path he turned angrily on me. "And your father too! It's time he moved over and let *you* run Marsden Manor. What was in his mind when he handed Jane's part of the woods to those Puritans?"

I had no answer. As we left the garden, the fog, drifting in from the sea ten miles away, was thicker than ever. We walked along the damp and rutted path and could have been anywhere. I felt I could stretch out a hand and push the fog aside like a curtain. Meg was looking down at the path beneath our feet. She was looking for the footprints that came from the churchyard gate, otherwise we'd have walked straight past it. She tugged my sleeve and led me towards the wooden gate.

It was open. The church loomed ahead of us, just a darker grey shape in the mist. At either side of the path there were mounds of earth where villagers had been buried. A few had rotting wooden crosses with forgotten names worn away. Others had a stone lying over the grave or standing at one end. Yellow moss covered some of the older ones.

Nearest to the church there was a large marble tomb like a small house. Grandfather stopped and looked at it

for a long time. It was the Marsden family tomb. All the people I had heard about in the family stories were lying under there. The thought made me shudder.

Grandfather smiled suddenly. "Let's go and look at this new grave, shall we? The one where they found coal. The "black gold" they call it!"

"The grave's been filled in," Meg said. "Old Tom the Tanner was buried there yesterday."

"No, they dug him a *new* grave. The grave they were digging when they struck a coal seam is still open, I believe. People from the village have been sneaking in to get themselves some free fuel!" said Grandfather, with a chuckle.

"They're there now," Meg whispered.

"I can't see anything," I said.

"But you can hear. Listen!"

I strained my ears and heard the scrape of iron on earth. In the dead dampness of the air it was hard to tell which direction it was coming from or how far away it was. Meg pointed, took two steps forward ... and vanished.

I thought at first she'd been swallowed by the mist, but that was impossible. I crept forward, one step at a time. I heard her groan. Then I felt the ground crumble under my toes and looked down. I was on the edge of a crude pit. It was the grave where coal had been found. Now it had been enlarged by scavengers after a share of the black gold.

Meg was lying on her back, staring up at me with a shocked face. Then her eyes narrowed and she hissed, "Don't you dare!"

"Dare what?"

"Laugh!"

"I wasn't!"

"You want to."

"I don't!" I lied and buried my face in my cloak.

"Help me out, you … you Marsden monster."

I reached down and took her hand. She gripped the edge of the pit and it crumbled away in her hand. But one piece of hard black rock stayed. She kept it in her right hand as I pulled her up by the other. Meg held it above her head and aimed to bring it down on my skull. "You're laughing!" she hissed between her teeth.

"I'm smiling … I am so pleased to see you're not hurt. I'm *smiling*, Meg. Happy for you."

She lowered the black rock and looked at it. Then she wiped some of the earth from it and forced it into a pocket in her dress. "What is it?" Grandfather asked.

Then, from somewhere to our right the digging stopped

and we heard voices. "Ghosts!" I whispered.

"No such thing," Meg murmured. "Men. Let's get closer and hear what they say."

We stepped carefully around the pit and over mounds of old graves. The voices were louder now and I was glad to see a large headstone that we could hide behind. The voices were muffled by the mist, but I knew them and I could make out what they were saying.

"Let's put the body by the grave," Luther Ramsbottom said.

There was a sound of dragging and a rattle as stones fell into an open grave. "Grave-robbers," Meg whispered.

"Why would anyone want to rob a grave?" I asked.

"For magic," she replied. "Hush!"

"This is the body of Tom Tanner," said Luther Ramsbottom, his deep voice as hollow as a grave.

"I see that," a young woman replied. That was the voice of the witness against Jane Atkinson! It was young Sarah White, the milkmaid.

"The spirit of the newly dead will still be in the graveyard," Ramsbottom said.

"Will it?" the girl squawked.

"For just a little while. Long enough to talk to it through a medium like me."

"I'm scared," the girl said. "This is witchcraft, just like they're going to hang Jane Atkinson for!"

"It is not witchcraft. You are in a churchyard with the servant of the holy Calvin Cartwright. Witchcraft is speaking with *evil* spirits. But in a place like this there are only *angels*!"

"Are you sure?" asked Sarah.

"Ask your question and I will see if the spirit will answer you," said the fat little Puritan.

"Will I get to marry Bartholomew Ironsmith?" asked Sarah.

A high, wavering voice came from somewhere near the corner of the church. "You will if you serve the church well." Of course, the second voice came from Knox Brodie, hidden in the fog.

"Oooh!" the girl moaned.

"It's all right, Sarah. That was a good angel."

"And I'm a green goblin," Meg murmured.

"How will I marry Bartholomew when he's already married to Ginny?" the girl asked.

"Perhaps she'll die!" the voice replied.

"Will she?"

"She will ... if you are *good.*"

There was a short silence. Then Sarah went on, "What do I have to do?"

"Speak out against the witch in Marsden Hall."

"Jane Atkinson? I already done that," she said.

"But Jane Atkinson has not been hanged. Satan's servants in the hall are protecting her. You must get rid of the sinners in Marsden Hall before Marsden Village will thrive again."

"Who are they?" Sarah asked.

Somehow I felt sure that the voice was going to accuse my grandmother, Jane's old friend who had met the famous John Dee and stuck pins in a wax doll. If *that* story was told outside Marsden Hall, Grandmother might hang alongside Widow Atkinson. I waited for the voice to say, "Lady Eleanor Marsden'. I wasn't prepared for what it *did* say.

"Witch Atkinson was in the grasp of Calvin Cartwright this morning," the hidden Puritan said. He was losing the wavering tone and anger was coming through. "She should have burned with her house the way we planned. Burning is *better* for witches. But she was rescued by two children of the Devil. Satan sent them at that moment to ruin our plans. Now they must be destroyed with Witch Atkinson."

"Will Marsden and Meg Lumley!" the girl cried. "They are the ones!"

"What have they done?"

"The boy is an actor. He dresses as a woman, he disguises himself as people who died many years ago. He steps on stage and makes those people live again. It's worse than raising up the dead. How can their spirits rest when this boy and his fellows make them live again on stage. It's sin, it's sin, it's sin!" the voice chanted.

"It is!" Sarah cried.

"Of course the Meg girl helps him."

"What does she do?"

There was a pause. The "angel" voice answered irritably, "I'm sure that you'll find something. Spread the word among the folk of Marsden Village. They will give you all the facts you need to bring them both to trial. Go to the Black Bull Tavern tonight and spread the word."

"I will," Sarah promised. "But when will I get to marry Bartholomew?"

"When you have done your duty to your church and your village. Now place the body of Tom the Tanner back in his resting place and help my friend cover him over."

"Your friend?"

"I meant ... I meant my medium."

"I see," the girl said.

We heard them working quickly on the grave, then shrank behind the headstone as the girl's voice came nearer to us, saying, "Good day, Master Ramsbottom ... and thanks!"

She rustled past us, her skirts trailing in the long damp grass. Moments later there was a scream. "Who's there?" called Ramsbottom. He sounded frightened.

"It's me!" sobbed Sarah the Milkmaid.

"Get back to work!"

"I'm trying. But I fell into this pit! I hurt my knee!"

"Then you'll have to hop out," said Ramsbottom, in a low angry voice. "But get out of here before anyone sees you."

The girl's snivels and groans faded as she made her way out of the graveyard.

When everything was quiet again I heard Luther Ramsbottom say, "It worked then?"

"It worked," Knox Brodie agreed. "We get young Marsden on trial and the family will do anything to save him from the rope."

"Anything," his 'brother' said. "Even give us the rest of Bournmoor Woods."

"Hah! At the very least. Maybe some of their mines and ships."

"They can afford it," Ramsbottom said bitterly.

The voices of the men faded as they walked away behind the church. I was shaking, more with anger than fear, and I could see from Meg's face that she felt the same. But as Grandfather slowly straightened himself, he was looking thoughtful. We picked our way carefully between the graves and headed back for Marsden Hall.

When we were in front of the fire in the hall, Meg brought hot wine from the kitchens and we supped at it. "Should we tell Calvin Cartwright what those two rogues are up to?" I asked.

"Not yet," Grandfather said. "It would look as if you were trying to escape from the charge of witchcraft. You have no witnesses."

"Sarah White," I said.

"She wouldn't admit to digging up Tom Tanner and speaking to an angel."

"But *you* were there!" Meg said eagerly. "They'd *have* to believe you!"

"No. I am a friend of Widow Atkinson as well as the grandfather of one of the accused. They wouldn't believe me. They would probably accuse *me* of being a witch too."

"Doesn't that frighten you?" I asked.

He shrugged. "I'm like Queen Elizabeth. I have been on this earth too long and it's time I made space for the young to take over. I'm not afraid to die – in my bed or at the end of a rope. But I have spent my life trying to make Marsden Manor a fit place for my grandson and all the great – grandchildren I'll never see. No, Will, I'm not afraid for myself. But I am afraid for the future of Marsden Hall."

"The villagers won't speak out against Meg and Me," I tried to argue.

He looked at me sadly. "They *would*. They hate your father because he has been a harsh magistrate. They see Meg as an adopted child of the same family – and you *are*, in a way, Meg. They are jealous. That's what this is all about. Jealousy."

"And it was jealousy made Princess Elizabeth want her stepsister's throne," Meg said, staring into the fire.

"As long as you are here you are in danger," Grandfather said. "Once Sarah White starts spreading her rumours, the witch-hunters will want your blood."

"So what do we do?"

"Do what you always planned. Go to London. Work for Master Shakespeare, perform for the Queen."

"We can't leave Widow Atkinson in danger," Meg said and her face was flushed by the heat of the fire and her anger.

"I'll take care of her," Grandfather said. "The old ones will look after each other. And you young ones have to do the same."

"When can we come home?" I asked.

My grandfather closed his eyes and rested his head against the back of his chair. "When Queen Elizabeth dies," he said.

"That may be five years – ten years!" I cried in dismay. "Why wait till then?"

He looked at me with tired eyes. "The villagers hate us in times of peace. But when danger comes – especially when the Scots march south – they turn to us to lead them. Great-Uncle George and I are too old. Your father is no soldier. But you will be their new young hero." He looked up at the figures carved into the stone of the mantelpiece – the Marsden family emblem. A knight slaying a dragon. "Go away as the wicked witch, but return as the new Saint George."

"Do I have to go away so long?" I'd imagined I'd work for Master Shakespeare in the winter, but return home every summer. I never dreamed I'd be going into exile.

"I'll write to you," Grandfather said. "Every time one of the Marsden ships takes coal to London there'll be a letter on board for you."

"And for me?" Meg asked.

He nodded. "Lady Marsden will miss you. She'll probably want to write to you every day, Meg. Don't worry."

"Is there no other way?" I asked.

"While the Puritans are poisoning the minds of the people it is not safe. You heard them. They will threaten you to get their hands on Marsden Manor – or they will hang you and Marsden Manor will be lost to the Marsden family anyway. No, Will, you are safer in London. You're packed to leave today. Go now and wait on the ship at Wearmouth till the weather changes."

"Have I time to say goodbye to everyone?" I asked.

"Not too long, Will. Time is short for all of us."

I didn't quite understand what he meant. Not then. But I felt a clock ticking away inside me as I hurried upstairs to my grandmother's room.

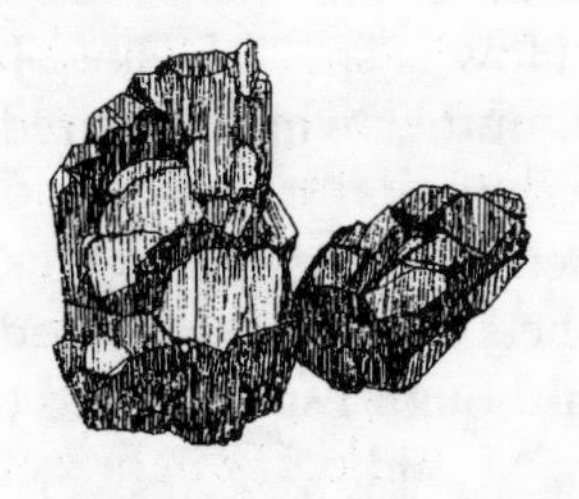

Chapter Six

"Both sovereign power and father's voice I have to use"

I can still remember the smell of sickness in that room. For all the sweetness of Jane Atkinson's herbs, the scent of something more dreadful made me want to retch. I am ashamed of myself now – I should have given my suffering grandmother all the time she wanted – but in truth I just wanted to escape to the fresh air of the North Sea.

The light outside was growing brighter as a faint breeze began to blow away the mist. Widow Atkinson hung a red cloth at the window. "The light hurts her eyes," she explained. "And they say that red light helps the healing."

Everything in the room was tinted with a ghastly shade of blood red. "How is she?" I asked Jane Atkinson.

It was Grandmother who answered. "*Old.* That's how she is and how she feels."

"You'll get better," Meg said. "You're strong."

"Perhaps," she said. "Sit on my bed."

We obeyed, although I still wanted to run. "We're going to London now," I said.

"You've missed the tide," she said. Her body was frail, but her mind was as sharp as ever.

"We'll wait on the ship for tomorrow's tide," I said. "We need to get away from Marsden Manor for a while. Till all this witchcraft nonsense dies down."

Grandmother chuckled softly. "You think you'll be safer

with the Queen, do you? Remember she's ruthless. A spoiled child and a spoiled queen. She has to have her own way. If she doesn't get what she wants, someone suffers. I could tell you stories about Queen Elizabeth that would get me executed if they went outside this room."

"Tell us one," Meg said.

"We have to get away, Meg," I said.

"If the fog's lifting, then we need to wait till dark. It may not be safe for us to be out on the Marsden roads in daylight. Anyway, your grandmother's more important than your trip to London."

Even in the faded light Meg's eyes burned fiercely. I sat and I listened.

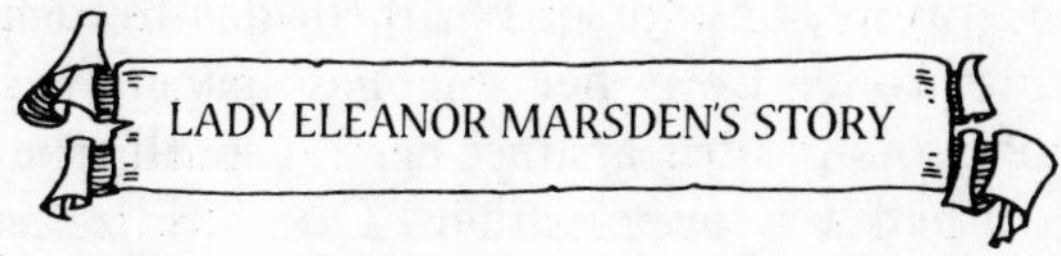

After the misery of Mary's reign, the people were so pleased to see their new queen. And she pretended to be so pleased with them. "I will be a good queen," she said at her coronation.

When her mother Anne Boleyn was crowned there had been some feeble applause and even some jeering. But Queen Elizabeth was cheered every inch from her lodging in the Tower of London to her crowning in Westminster Abbey. She was carried in a chair covered in yellow cloth of gold and the people were dazzled by her splendour. And, for all her rotting teeth and orange wigs and lead-painted face, they still are.

She did a strange thing to make sure that the coronation was a success, you know. She called in Doctor John Dee and asked him to cast a horoscope. He had to say which was the best day for her to be crowned. Dee said the stars would be best on the fifteenth of January and that was the day she chose.

Dee was right, of course. Elizabeth has lived long and kept her throne. Even her enemies helped her! Mary Queen of Scots plotted against her ... so all true English people rushed to support their Queen Elizabeth. The Spanish sent a great Armada ... so all true English people supported their Queen Elizabeth. Oh, the plots I could tell you about! Sometimes I wonder if Elizabeth didn't make up some of the plots against herself just to keep her popularity!

But the one thing Dee *couldn't* give the Queen was a husband and a child to take her throne when she dies. And that's why there's all this misery now.

Of course Dee didn't have to mix a love potion for Elizabeth. She was loved by kings and princes and lords. So, why did she never marry? I'll tell you what I think – and I should know, because I was there. I think she has always loved Robert Dudley.

If I hadn't been married I could have loved the man myself! Oh, but he was handsome. I remember the day he strode into the palace.

"Who's that?" I asked John Dee.

Doctor Dee always dressed plainly in black, but Robert

Dudley could afford the best tailor in London and the finest materials in the world. The first time I saw him he was in purple velvet. Queen Elizabeth was a wise woman, but she was always stirred by fine clothes. We ladies-in-waiting would never have dared dress in fine clothes in case we outshone her. But a man in rich clothes made her blood run hot.

"That is the son of a traitor," Dee said sourly.

"What's his name?" I asked, as the young man swept off his feathered hat and knelt before the Queen.

"He's one of the Dudley family. His grandfather tried to rob Henry VII and was executed by Henry VIII. And his father, the Duke of Northumberland, tried to put Lady Jane Grey on the throne instead of Queen Mary. He lost his head too. Traitors and deceivers all," Dee sneered.

"Don't you like the Dudley family, then?" I teased.

He looked at me and curled his nose as if I'd used cow dung for perfume. "Women seem to like him," he said.

The Queen's ladies close to the throne were giggling and blushing as Robert Dudley was introduced to each one in turn. "And this is Lady Eleanor Marsden," the Queen said, smiling.

"It's an honour to meet someone so beautiful," he said, and I have to admit I blushed, although I was much older than the giggling girls around him.

The Queen's smile vanished. "Is Lady Eleanor more beautiful than your queen?" she asked lightly. The laughter stopped and everyone seemed to hold their breath.

"Lady Eleanor is as beautiful as a violet. On her own she is as fair as any flower. But, next to a royal rose like Your Majesty, even a violet looks dull and ordinary!"

The Queen was pleased with the reply and everyone breathed again. Of course I was *so* pleased at being called dull and ordinary, you can imagine, I could happily have taken his jewelled dagger and pushed it through his jewelled doublet.

They chatted for an hour or more on that visit. Messengers came from ministers and were sent away. The next day the Queen went hunting with her new admirer and he was invited back again every day. They listened to music and talked of books and horses and fashions and wine and poetry.

They were never to be left alone together, Queen Elizabeth made that quite clear. "We cannot have idle gossips saying Lord Dudley and I are *too* close," she said.

But the gossips prattled when she was out of sight. "She loves him," Lady Jane Horsley said one summer evening, as we sat in the garden while Doctor Dee studied the stars.

"I think she should marry him," Kate Ashley said. Kate was always more serious than the others. "It is not respectable."

John Dee turned from his astronomical instruments and

said, "And what would the good Dudley do with the wife he already has? Are you suggesting the Queen should share his handsome figure with Amy Robsart?"

"I've heard Amy is ill," Kate said. "She has chest pains. Perhaps she'll die."

Dee frowned and said, "That's an interesting thought. I must cast a horoscope for Dudley and his wife."

Jane Horsley gasped. "The Queen would never allow it!"

"The Queen would not need to know," he said quietly.

"When will you do it?"

"Tonight. The time of their births will be recorded in the rolls in the palace. I'll find them and look into their future."

"And will you tell us what you see in the stars?" Jane asked excitedly.

"Perhaps," he said, then seemed unwilling to say more.

But, next morning, when we had eaten breakfast in the palace hall and dragged John Dee into a side room, he refused to tell us anything. "I am not free to tell you Her Majesty's secrets," he said.

"You promised!" said Jane.

"I did not," he reminded her sternly.

"So it's bad? Is there a death in the stars?"

Dee didn't say anything. "That means "yes'," Kate said quietly.

"I think the Queen will grow tired of Dudley and have him executed," said Jane, gripping her pale throat.

But Jane was wrong. We were all wrong ... except, perhaps, John Dee. The news when it arrived was more shocking than anyone suspected. It came after a week when the Queen and Dudley had spent all their time shut up together. Sometimes I was the only lady-in-waiting present. I busied myself with my sewing and couldn't hear their secret conversations.

Everyone was turned away at the door. If the King of

Spain had landed with an invading army that week, I think the Queen would have said, "Tell him to go away, I'm busy."

There was one messenger who did get through. Kate tapped on the door and entered the Queen's private room. She was sitting in the window seat with Dudley and looked up furiously. Kate dropped a low curtsey and stayed on her knee. "Your Majesty … it is a messenger from Cumnor Place."

"My home?" Dudley said. "Excuse me, Your Majesty. Amy must have some message for me."

"Nothing too secret for me to hear," the Queen said tartly. "Let him enter," she said to Kate.

The man came into the room, his boots thick with dust from the summer roads and with no time to clean them before coming before the Queen. "Well, man, what is it?" Dudley asked. He was charming enough with the Queen and her ladies, but a harsh master to the menservants.

"It's your wife, sir."

"What about her? Is she well?"

"No, sir. She's dead."

"Dead!" the Queen said. Just for a moment I saw a flash of satisfaction in her eyes. Then she covered her face with an expression of sorrow. "Oh, Robert! I am so sorry. I never realized she was so ill. Perhaps you should have been with her."

"She didn't die of her illness," said the messenger. His voice was little more than a whisper.

Dudley grabbed him roughly by the arm. "What then?"

"An accident. She was found at the bottom of the main staircase. The doctor said her neck had been broken."

Queen Elizabeth sat down suddenly and Dudley let go of the man's arm. "An accident, you say? How did she fall?"

"No one knows. The servants were all out of the house at the time. She was alone."

"No!" the Queen cried. Her nimble brain had seen what that meant. For the only time in her life she spoke carelessly in front of me. "You see what this means. They'll say it was no accident. They'll say she was pushed."

"Murdered? Who would want to murder Amy?" Dudley cried.

Queen Elizabeth looked up at him with some contempt. "They will say that *I* wanted her dead, you fool. They will blame me."

"No ..."

"Get out. Get away from the palace and back to Cumnor. If your stupid wife had died peacefully in her bed, then all would have been well for us. But this changes everything."

"You can marry me now," Dudley said in a low voice.

"I can *never* marry you," she said bitterly. She turned her back on him and looked out of the window over the dazzling gardens. "I will never marry anyone."

That was the moment when the future of England changed. Once my mistress decided she would never marry, never have an heir to the English throne, she changed the course of history.

Dudley was sent away. After a week she remembered that I had been in the room when the message was brought. She called me to her and said, "It's time you went home to Marsden Manor, Eleanor. I have made you neglect your husband ... and you have a child."

"A son. James."

"I'll never have a husband or a son," she said coldly. "But you will be well rewarded for your service to me."

"Thank you, Your Majesty."

Then her mood changed from coldness to fury and I saw her father's madness flash in her eyes. "But if you ever repeat the wicked stories they are spreading, I will have you and your precious son thrown into the darkest room in the Tower, of London."

There was no need for her to threaten me. I was no traitor. But she was terrified that the people of England would blame her for Amy Robsart's death. So terrified that she sent her spies out into the country to listen to the tavern gossips. They found plenty. There was one in Durham who spread stories about the Queen, and he had his head put in a pillory. A paper crown was placed on his head with the words, "This man told lies about the Queen." His ears were nailed to the pillory and then sliced off.

The rumours stopped and in time Dudley went back to the Queen's court. But she knew she could never marry him. She was determined never to marry anyone.

My grandmother's voice was becoming weaker, but she went on, "Queen Elizabeth didn't murder the women who stood in her way – she didn't have her sister Mary poisoned or Amy Robsart pushed. But it's strange how those poor creatures died when Elizabeth wanted them to."

"You think the Queen has the power to curse people?" Meg asked.

"Doctor Dee was a clever man. He really did seem to see into the future. Before I left the court and came home he did my horoscope. He said I'd have no more children, but I would have a grandson. He said I'd live as long as the Queen."

"You've lived longer," I said. "You're already older than she is and she's dying."

"That isn't what Dee meant," she said. "I think he meant that while she lives, I will live."

I shivered. "And when she dies?"

"Nobody lives for ever," said my grandmother. "But you can live longer if you take heed of what I'm saying. Queen Elizabeth likes handsome men around her. Dudley – and then the Earl of Essex – she can raise them up to great heights and she can destroy them just as easily."

"Yes, Grandmother."

Her face creased in a frown. "You don't understand what I'm saying, do you?"

"He's only a boy," Meg reminded her. I glared across

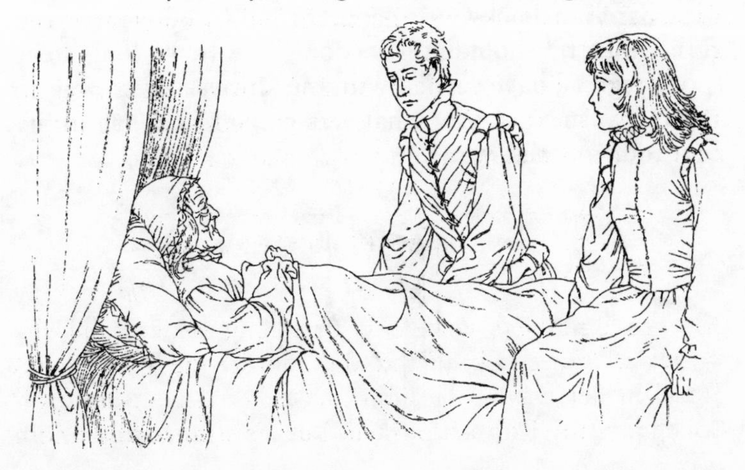

the bed at her and she smiled back innocently. "Your grandmother is warning you against the Queen. If she takes a fancy to you when you perform for her, she can make your fortune."

"Me?" I gasped.

"Don't be *completely* stupid, Will," she said. "You're a handsome young man and the Queen still imagines herself a beautiful woman."

I shook my head, bewildered.

"The spoilt Queen always gets her own way," Grandmother said. "But if you are prepared for her, then you might just be the first man to get the better of her."

"I still don't understand," I said.

Grandmother groaned and lay back on her pillows. Meg leaned across to me. "Lady Eleanor means that you can get what you want from the Queen if you use your charms – and, if you're cunning, you won't be destroyed by her."

"Get what I want? What do I want?"

"You want to save Jane Atkinson's neck from the gallows – and you may just save your own and mine while you're at it."

I was so horrified at the thought that I left the bedroom with barely a backward glance or a "Goodbye" to my grandmother. I shouldn't have done that. In my long life it is one regret I have carried with me always.

But I wasn't to know what was going to happen in the next four months, was I?

Chapter Seven

"I know my business is but to the court"

When I walked downstairs into the hall I thought I was walking into another trial. In a way I was. My grandfather and Great-Uncle George were sitting behind the table while my father and Calvin Cartwright sat facing them as a pair of prisoners would. Father looked uncomfortable. Calvin Cartwright looked scornful.

"William here can help us!" Great-Uncle George cried, as I walked in.

"Help what?"

"With this problem of Widow Atkinson."

"The witchcraft?" I asked.

"No. The poor woman losing her cottage. Your father here has made a mistake. He thought she held the cottage as a tenant-at-will. That means he could throw her out at any time and take back her land."

"So what *is* she?" Calvin Cartwright asked.

Great-Uncle George ignored him and turned to me. "Your grandfather and I have been looking at the Marsden estate documents and we discovered that Widow Atkinson's husband was a leaseholder."

I shook my head. I knew about the criminal cases that came before the magistrates, but all this talk of land and property confused me.

Grandfather explained patiently. “Leaseholders are protected by the law. No one can take the land off them while they live there.”

My father’s face was purple with anger. “There is another, *greater* law. It says that a married woman cannot own land! As soon as she marries, everything she owns becomes her husband’s. Widow Atkinson was a tenant-at-will. *My* will. I let her stay there because I am tender-hearted and care for my old tenants.”

Grandfather jabbed a sharp finger at him. “James, you are talking pompous drivel. You care for James Marsden and no one else!”

“That’s not fair, Father!”

“And, not only are you mean and selfish, you are also ignorant! You were at sea with Sir Francis Drake when Jane Atkinson’s husband died. But I was running this estate in your absence. John Atkinson was the leaseholder. And there is a custom known as “widow-right’. According to that custom Jane, as a widow, was allowed to stay on the land as a leaseholder for the rest of her natural life. She is *not* one of your tenants-at-will.”

My father’s colour drained. “Widow-right? You should have said before.”

“I didn’t have these documents this morning,” Grandfather said. “I do now.”

“So the deal with Calvin Cartwright and the Puritans is off?” I asked. “We can’t exchange Widow Atkinson’s corner of Bournmoor Woods for the graveyard land?”

“It’s all signed and sealed, and you have given your word!” said Cartwright coldly.

“And her cottage has already been destroyed,” I reminded them. My father gave me a look like a poisoned dagger.

“Calvin Cartwright must give back the land to Widow Atkinson,” Grandfather said firmly. “And Calvin Cartwright must pay her one hundred pounds to build a new house."

"I won't do that," Cartwright said with a harsh laugh. "Sir James handed that land over to me in a legal deal."

"You cheated him, you crop-haired, sour-faced serpent," Great-Uncle George said angrily. "He thought he was getting the church land with all its coal. You forgot to tell my greedy nephew that the church will not give him permission to dig on holy ground. Will it? He exchanged some of the finest woodland in Durham for a heap of crumbling bones."

Father's jaw dropped. "Is that true, Calvin?" he asked.

The Puritan gave a single nod.

I thought my father was going to burst into tears. "Cheated! You cheated me!"

"Only because you thought you would make a fortune from the coal. You are a sinner who was cheated by his own greed. You exchanged your patch of forest for a churchyard because you believed *you* were cheating *me*!"

"I want that land in Bournmoor Woods back," said Father.

"And my church will not hand it back."

"You will have to if the Queen's Star Chamber orders you," Grandfather said.

"The Star Chamber? Widow Atkinson can't go to London," said my father.

"No, but you can, James," Great-Uncle George said smugly. "We have gathered all the documents. You must deliver them to our friend, Robert Carey, and Carey will present them to the Star Chamber."

Calvin Cartwright rose to his feet. "If it's a battle in the Queen's Star Chamber you want, then that's what you shall have," he said. "But, remember, Widow Atkinson is going to hang as a witch anyway. I wouldn't be surprised if your serving girl and your son stood on the scaffold alongside her. Then you may be glad to give me a little patch of woodland in exchange for your son's life," he said. He placed his hat firmly on his head and strode to the door and out into the dull afternoon.

I sat in Cartwright's seat and pulled it close to the table. "Can he do that?" I asked.

"Unless you get a royal pardon," Grandfather said. "Jane Atkinson has been held for trial at the assizes now. With the mood of people in the village they could well hang her. And you and Meg could suffer with her if the assizes look for her fellow-witches on the manor. I've seen it happen before."

"So where will we get a royal pardon?" I asked.

"Why, from the Queen herself," Great-Uncle George said. "Your grandmother did her some service when your grandfather and I were fighting on the Scottish Borders for her. Your father served against the Spanish Armada. She may remember. The Marsdens have been loyal servants to the crown."

I thought about this. "So, I have to go to London and work for Master Shakespeare. Then I have to persuade the Queen to pardon Jane Atkinson. Is that all?"

Grandfather raised one eyebrow. "That's all."

"What should I do on my *second* day in London?" I asked.

Great-Uncle George leaned across the table and glared at me with mock fierceness. "That is an insolent way to speak to your old relations. I think you are learning a sharp tongue from that girl Meg."

"I think perhaps I need it," I sighed.

I rose from the chair and began to gather my baggage for the sea trip to London. I packed my play scripts and my clean linen, some money and some writing materials.

Meg came from the kitchens with her bundle. She was frowning.

"What's wrong?" I asked.

"Constable Smith came to the kitchen door a little while ago. He says the villagers haven't gone back to work since Jane Atkinson's hearing this morning."

"They won't be paid," my father said sharply. He had a roll of sea charts and his navigation instruments packed, ready to go.

"They've been drinking at the Black Bull and they're in a troublesome mood."

"Jane Atkinson is safe enough in the house. We'll tell Grandfather to lock the main gates behind us. That's enough to keep the drunken rabble out."

Meg took a deep breath. "It's not just Jane they're after. Sarah White has been in the tavern and stirring up trouble for Jane's friends."

"What friends?" Father asked. "You don't want me to bring all the old woman's cronies into the shelter of Marsden Hall too, do you?"

"They're already here," Meg said. "It is Master William and me that they want now. They know we helped Jane this morning. They think we're in league with her and the Devil. They want to duck us to find out."

Father nodded. Now he saw the problem. "It could be tricky getting from here to the boats at Wearmouth. Perhaps we should wait until dark."

Meg shook her head. "We have to ride along the river bank. At this time of year the fog can roll in from the river when the sun sets. We'd be riding completely blind. They could simply wait for us on Fatfield Bridge. Once we were on the bridge they could block off both ends and we'd be trapped."

It sounded like a good plan. "You have a criminal mind, Meg Lumley," I said.

"I must get it from the family I'm living with."

Luckily Father didn't hear that. "We'll have to leave at once," he said.

"We're easier targets in the daylight," I said. "But at least Constable Smith will be able to protect us."

"Hah!" Father said with a harsh laugh. "Constable Smith would be torn apart by the mob. We'd need a troop of soldiers from Durham Castle to get us out of here safely. We're like a castle under siege!"

"I could go ahead and talk to them," Meg offered. "After all, I'm one of them."

Father gripped her shoulders suddenly and said, "Not any more, Meg Lumley. I think they will see you as a Marsden now." My father could be cruel and stupid.

Then, at moments like that, he surprised me and made me think there was hope for him.

"So? What do we do?"

"We head south-west to Chester-le-Street, then turn east along the other bank of the Wear. They won't be expecting that," he said.

It was a plan with a fair chance of success. "I don't like running from my own home like a criminal," I said.

"It's only until you get that pardon from the Queen. The people still believe what her father, Henry, told them – the Tudors are God's chosen leaders. If the Queen pardons Widow Atkinson, then the villagers will."

"I'll be banished from Marsden till then?" I asked. We had never been popular in the village, but I hadn't imagined it would come to this.

"Let's hope the Queen lives long enough to grant a pardon," my father said.

I shook my head. "I thought everyone wanted her dead?"

"Yes . . . but not yet. Not quite yet!" He straightened his stooped shoulders, hunched from years of bending over account books and law books and estate records. I'd seen my father captaining his ship under attack and it brought him to life. He buckled on his sword and seemed to grow another inch again. "Shall we chance it now?" he asked. The mean, money-counting, quill-pushing magistrate had the Marsden family blood somewhere in his veins.

Meg grinned. She was happier than I'd seen her for weeks. "Can I take a sword?" she asked eagerly. "I'd only use the flat to crack their skulls. I wouldn't use it to slice or stab."

Father frowned. "Only a gentleman carries a sword."

"A pistol, then?"

"And only a robber carries a pistol. It is against the law to carry a pistol on the highways. What sort of rogue are you, Meg Lumley?" he asked sternly.

"A very useful one in a fight," she sniffed.

"Take a wooden quarterstaff," I suggested.

She pulled a disappointed face, but went to the armoury to find something suitable. I hurried after her. "I'll have a crossbow," I said.

"Longbows are better," she said, as we hurried down the dim corridors. There was enough daylight to see our way through the house and it was still too early to waste good candles to light Marsden Hall. "Great-Uncle George is always telling us stories of how the English longbows beat the crossbows in the wars against the French."

I had had enough training in weapons to be able to argue with her for once. "That was for the archers on foot," I explained. "They're too difficult to handle when you're on horseback. On horseback the crossbow is king."

Meg had no answer to this. I felt almost dizzy with the success of winning an argument with her. I selected a well-greased crossbow and six sharp, iron-tipped bolts. Just one well-aimed bolt could bring down a stag. I'd hate to think what it might do to a man's head. I felt better with it in my hand.

I turned from the armoury and locked the door behind me. Meg followed me and, somehow, her oak quarterstaff became entangled with my legs and I crashed to my knees, my crossbow gouging splinters from the wooden floor. Meg stepped over me and let the end of the staff catch my ear. "On horseback the crossbow is king," she mimicked. "But in the corridors of Marsden Hall the quarterstaff is queen."

I struggled up on my bruised knees, cursed her, and vowed never to win an argument with her again.

I limped out of the side door into the stable yard. Martin the Ostler already had the hall's best horses saddled and was fastening on our saddle packs. "It's getting late to be riding for Wearmouth," he said. The sky was as dull as lead and a mist was swirling slowly through the tops of the distant trees. "The mist is coming off the river."

"It's all right," Meg said. "We're heading north. We're taking a ship from the Tyne!"

I looked at her, puzzled. She stepped closer to me and said softly, "Trust nobody."

"But Martin!" I hissed. "He's been with the family all his life!"

"And where does his mother live?" Meg asked.

"I don't know."

"By the church. Next door to Sarah White, as it happens. If his mother tells him that he's working for witches, who knows what he'll do?"

"Martin wouldn't betray us," I whispered angrily.

"I'll remind you of those words when we have hemp ropes round our necks and a ladder under our feet, shall I?" she replied equally furiously. "Just before they turn us off." Her sea-green eyes burned for an instant and then softened. "Sorry, Will. There's just no need for us to take any more risks than we have to."

I managed a smile. "You're right."

My mother came out of the house with cloaks for Meg and me. Grandfather and Great-Uncle George stood behind her in the doorway. They looked grim. "I wish I were ten years younger," my great-uncle sighed.

"You'd be more use if you were fifty years younger," Grandfather told him.

"Aye, that's true. The old have to make way for the young at some time."

"Tell that to Queen Elizabeth," Grandfather said. "That's what this trouble is really about. Uncertain people are frightened people."

"We'll survive," Father said. He and Grandfather had never shared any love – not that I'd seen. But now they stepped forward at the same moment and clasped one another with muttered words of "good luck" and "take care'.

Then it was Great-Uncle George's turn, while Grandfather moved towards me. He put his arms around me and I was smothered by the musty fur collar of his robe. I felt tears prick in my eyes. I can still recall that smell and it still makes me too sad for words. I remembered one of the lines from Master Shakespeare's *Romeo and Juliet* and murmured it, "'Farewell! God knows when we shall meet again.'"

"What was that?" Grandfather asked.

"Nothing," I mumbled.

"Take care of my friend Meg," he said.

"I think she thinks she's coming along to take care of me!" I said, and laughed.

He smiled, his faded eyes lost in the wrinkles. "I think you're right," he said.

We mounted and clattered over the cobbles of the stable yard. Father had a superstition that a sailor leaving port should never look back. But I wasn't a sailor in port and I risked it anyway. My mother was watching, pale and calm, from a window in the tower. Grandfather and Great-Uncle George looked more anxious, but I knew they were not so much worrying about us as envying us. Even at their great age they longed for danger and excitement.

Meg and I waved back, then we turned and headed into all the danger and excitement they could want.

As soon as Martin the Ostler slammed the oak gate shut behind us we heard the sharp cry of a seagull.

"That's lucky at the start of a journey," I told my father.

"Only if it came from a seagull and not from some hidden watcher," he said.

"It was probably a signal to let the villagers know we'd left the safety of the Marsden Hall walls," Meg said and spurred her horse down the path between the workers' cottages.

Window shutters moved as we rode by although there was very little wind now. If they attacked us I was ready. It was the waiting I couldn't stand. If anyone was there they were invisible.

We reached the crossroads where we met the road from Chester-le-Street to Wearmouth. Instead of turning east towards Wearmouth we turned west towards Bournmoor Woods. Amongst the trees it was as dark as midnight, although the sky above us was a flat, light grey. But even in the darkness Meg saw something on the forest path ahead that made her groan, "Oh, no! What do we do now?"

Chapter Eight

'We'll make you some sport with the fox'

The bitter smell of burning still hung in the air as we reached Widow Atkinson's ruined cottage. One of the huge elm trees that had stood behind the house had been cut down. It had fallen through the remains of the charred walls, across her herb garden and on to the road through the wood.

A short stout man in black stood there. "Master Ramsbottom!" my father said. "It is an offence to obstruct Her Majesty's highway! Remove this tree at once."

Ramsbottom's small, wicked eyes glinted even in the dying light. "I've been pushing and pushing, but it just won't move!"

"What's it doing there?"

"We cut it down to clear our woods," said Ramsbottom. "We'll be building a fine new house here, a barn and a paddock for some cattle."

"You'll ruin the hunting," my father objected.

"That's not your problem any longer," said Ramsbottom. "They're not your woods."

"How are we supposed to get past?"

"This will be cleared by tomorrow noon."

My father didn't stay to argue, but turned his horse back towards the village and said, "We'll take the hunting track to the south." He turned down towards the river

and spurred his horse forward. Suddenly it stumbled and my father gave a cry as he was thrown over its head. He landed heavily on the ground. I reined back my horse and jumped down. As I ran towards him I tripped over the obstacle that had made the horse fall. There was a rope stretched across the path, tied to a tree on either side.

"It's a trap!" Meg cried. Before I could run back and unfasten my crossbow, a man stepped from the shadow of the trees. He was wearing a woollen cloak. The hood was raised and a cloth was wrapped around the bottom half of his face, so I couldn't make out who it was.

"Stand back!" I called to him. "This is highway robbery and you'll hang for it!" I drew the dagger from the back of my belt.

The man was carrying a quarterstaff. He swung it expertly, smashed it against my wrist and sent my dagger spinning into the trees. As I clutched at my wrist I felt the hot, damp body of a horse push me aside from the path. It was Meg, who had let her horse step carefully over the rope.

The man turned to face her. She had pulled her oak staff from the strap on the saddle and jumped to the ground. The man braced himself and held the staff straight out in front of him. "You can't fight him, Meg!" I said, as she stepped towards him.

"Have you never heard the story of David and Goliath?" she asked.

"Who won?" I asked.

"The one who cheated, of course," she said with a grin.

Her opponent said, "Witch!" The word was muffled behind the cloth.

"Watch!" replied Meg and spun the staff around one finger of her right hand. Then she spun it again till it was as blurred as a wasp's wing. She stretched her hand above her head and spun it in a flat circle. She threw it in a high arc towards the dull sky and caught it expertly. Then she threw the staff up till one end was balanced on her fingertips. The staff swayed towards the man and Meg followed it. It tilted backwards and she stepped back. Every time the staff moved Meg followed.

It was like watching a rope-walker at Chester-le-Street fair, almost overbalancing and somehow getting upright again. It was a juggling performance that had the man entranced. My father was sitting up and watching, open-mouthed. "Ahh!" Meg gasped as the staff tilted towards our attacker. She took three or four steps forward until she was within the staff's length of the man.

I wasn't expecting what happened next, so the man on

the path had no chance. Meg turned her hand. The end of the staff slipped off her fingertips. Before it had dropped six inches she wrapped her hand firmly around it, then brought it down so quickly it whistled in the still air. The whistle was followed by a sickening crack as it smashed on to the man's skull. He gasped in pain and shock.

His staff fell to the ground and he clutched at his head. Meg brought her staff round in a huge swing that was aimed to take off his head. But the first blow must have weakened the wood and, as it caught the man on his ear, her staff snapped clean in two. Meg bent to pick up the man's own weapon and finish him off, but he had turned and was crashing blindly through the undergrowth to the safety of the shadows.

Meg picked up the man's quarterstaff and held it above her head in triumph. "David and Goliath, all over again. If you can't win in a fair fight, you must cheat a little."

I almost felt sorry for our attacker. My father staggered to his feet. "Well done, Meg Lumley. I'm only sorry my son wasn't more help."

She sighed. "He's only a man. What do you expect?"

I was glad that the woodland shade hid my blushes. "Shall we carry on along this road?"

"I think so," my father said. "They probably left just one man here to guard it. But we'll take it more slowly."

I recovered my dagger, we remounted and rode on. When we reached the river we stopped. The path turned west to meet the London road. "They may have that covered," Meg said. "Perhaps we should turn east to the Wear bridge."

"There's no path that way," my father said.

"There are poachers' trails we can follow. They won't be expecting us to come from that direction."

"How do you know about poachers' trails, young Meg?" my father asked sternly. I wasn't sure if he was teasing. It wasn't in his nature to tease.

But Meg answered him in a spirit of fun. "Villagers used to show me the river trails. They weren't really poachers, you know. The best salmon let themselves be caught by *your* cook, of course. They are *honoured* to be eaten by a Marsden. The salmon that aren't caught die of disappointment; they jump into the villagers' nets and give themselves up. It's not so much poaching. It's more keeping the river clear of sad salmon."

"Tshah!" my father spat disgustedly. "There aren't enough trees in Bournmoor Woods to hang all the villains in Marsden Manor."

We let Meg lead us along a muddy trail that wound between trees and through brambles. The river was on our right and sometimes we could see it through the undergrowth. The only sounds were the crackle of dead twigs under our horses' hooves and the cries of squabbling crows above our heads.

The bridge would be the dangerous part of this journey. Meg raised a hand and stopped us. She slipped from the saddle and said, "I'll go ahead on foot and see if it's safe."

In spite of my cloak I shivered in the damp air from the river. Meg appeared suddenly in the gloom. "There are a dozen men and women at this end of the bridge. They're just off the track at each side of the road. I'm sure there are as many at the far side. When the signal comes they'll block the far end. The ones at this end will stop us going back and we'll be trapped."

"Maybe if we surprise them we can ride through before they know we're there," I suggested.

"And maybe they'll knock you off your horse and duck you in the river," Meg said.

"Have you a better idea?"

"I'm glad you asked," she said.

"I thought you might be."

"Do you want to hear it?"

"Have I got any choice?" I asked.

"It's risky, but it's our only chance. We have to get them all to one end of the bridge," she said.

"This end," my father said. "The north end."

"Maybe not. It would be easier for me to get the ones at this end to the far end. Then, when they've got their backs to us, we ride through and on to Wearmouth," she said.

"How will you do it?" I asked.

And Meg explained. Then she turned and walked through the thickest of the undergrowth, leaving my father holding her horse. The daylight was almost gone now and the river was hidden under a blanket of mist that was rising every minute. Her plan wouldn't have worked at noon, but in this light we had a chance. I also knew if it went wrong, that Meg would be the first to fall into their hands. I prepared my crossbow. I didn't want to kill anyone, but if they took Meg I knew I might have to.

My father loosened his sword and looked at me. "It's the cunning peasant blood in the girl that makes her so good at this," he said.

Every time I began to like my father he always had to spoil it by showing his arrogance.

After an age we heard the sound we'd been waiting for. The scream of a girl running down from the village to the bridge. "The witches!" she was crying over and over again. "We saw them flying over the river! They're on the south bank and heading this way! The witches!"

From our hiding place near the bridge we saw people in hooded cloaks climb from the ditches by the roadside and hurry on to the bridge. As they ran over to the far side, the screaming girl stood alone, urging them on. "Hurry! They'll get away!"

Her face was covered with a cloth, the same as the others, and she'd tried to disguise her voice, but it was

Meg and her plan had worked so far. The bridge was deserted and the villagers were at the far side, with their backs to us. We led the horses on to the road and Meg swung herself into the saddle. The noise of three horses clattering over a wooden bridge made some of the witch-hunters turn and run back to block the way. Meg screamed, "There they are! I can see them!"

It confused our enemies long enough to let us finish the crossing and get on to the Wearmouth road. One man got close enough to lash at father with a wooden pole. Father met it with his sword and the staff was cut through cleanly.

The villagers began to scream, "Witches! Kill them!" and my horse panicked at the uproar. It reared and spun round to face the mob that was rushing towards me.

They were bending down and scooping up stones as they ran. Some of them began throwing them from twenty paces or more. I felt a sharp pain in my shoulder as one struck me and almost knocked me out of the saddle.

"Come *on*, Will!" Meg was crying, but the horse was going sideways and backing towards a ditch.

Then a stone caught my horse on the nose and it

decided it was time to flee from the rabble. It turned and bolted down the Wearmouth road, bursting past Father and Meg as stones rained down on our backs. The horse was out of control and in a panic, but the road was climbing up from the river and the steepness slowed it down and made it tired.

By the time I was at Penshaw the animal was feeling the bit in its mouth and I slowed it to a walk so that the other two could catch me. "I didn't know it was a race!" Meg said, "or I'd have probably beaten you."

"Let's hope the villagers don't win the race to the ship," my father said quietly.

"We've outrun them," I said.

"Don't be foolish, boy. They know where we're headed. It's only eight miles to Wearmouth and they'll be there within half an hour of us," he said.

Behind us I could hear the baying of the angry mob. I knew how a hunted fox must feel. We rode on into the near-darkness. If the horses ran too fast they might stumble and break a leg. We went as fast as we dared. But the gloom that had been our friend on the bridge was our enemy now.

When we reached the heights at Penshaw the river below us was hidden by a thick mist. Ahead we could see lanterns on the masts of some of the ships in the harbour. "They'll catch us while we wait to sail," I said.

"Perhaps not," my father said. "We were aiming for this afternoon's high tide. There should be another one about midnight. We can get the ship's boat to tow us out to mid-stream and even out to the harbour mouth. The fog may hide us."

The horses splashed on through puddles and the road dropped down towards the river and the fog. The last two miles were slow going. Fog makes riding difficult and so does darkness. Together they made it impossible. We dismounted and led the animals. Sometimes we lost contact with one another as we walked blindly. There were times when I thought we'd walked ten miles and must be nearer the River Tyne than the Wear.

Then there was an orange glow in the darkness. As we approached we could make out a flickering torch, and we were rattling over the quayside cobbles. We made our way quickly to the Marsdens' collier ship, the *Hawk*, and unfastened our baggage. Father told the watchman to fetch Captain Walsh and he explained the need for us to leave immediately. Captain Walsh shook his head. "It'll be dangerous going out into mid-stream in this fog. Only an idiot would do that," he said.

"Why?" Father snapped.

"Someone may run into us!"

"But only if they were idiot enough to go into mid-stream too," Meg pointed out.

The captain scratched his head. "True."

"And nobody's idiot enough to do that, are they, Captain Walsh?" asked my father.

"They're not!" Captain Walsh agreed.

"So we'll be safe!" Meg cried.

"We will!" the captain smiled. Then the smile slid off his face as he wondered how he'd lost that argument. He was still scratching his head as he roused the crew and told them to make ready to tow the *Hawk* into mid-stream and wait for the night tide.

Meg hurried across the quayside to leave the horses in the livery stables at the back of the tavern.

"It'll be dangerous in this fog," said the ship's mate.

"Aha!" Captain Walsh said, waving a finger in the air. "Only an idiot would do it!"

"That's right," the mate agreed.

"And you're an idiot, aren't you?"

"No!"

"So we'll be safe!"

"Eh!" said the mate. "Say that again, Captain. It doesn't make sense!"

"It did when Meg Lumley said it," Captain Walsh grumbled and began to organize the crew.

The ship's boat was lowered and attached to the bow of the *Hawk* with a rope. I was looking anxiously across the quayside towards the Marsden road. I knew we'd been slowed down so much the witch-hunters couldn't be too far behind.

Meg ran across the cobbles and leapt up the gangplank. I pulled it up as soon as she'd crossed. The first mate cast off and gave orders for the boat crew to start towing us away from the quayside. Dark shadows were moving uncertainly on to the deserted quay. The villagers were arriving, but were uncertain where the *Hawk* had been moored.

We inched our way from land and the shapes seemed to sense the movement. They ran towards us. "Witch!" they cried. "Witch! Witch! Witch!"

As we left them behind in the orange fog we saw sailors spilling out of the taverns to see what the noise was about.

"What's all that about, then?" Captain Walsh asked.

"Some village nonsense," Father said. "Prepare our cabin."

"Ah! Problem there," Walsh said and rubbed his chins down towards his grubby collar. "Your cabin is ready, as ever, Sir James. But we weren't expecting Miss Meg. We've got a paying passenger in the spare cabin."

"It can't be helped," my father said. "Meg will have to sleep in a sail locker."

"Thanks," she said tartly. "I don't suppose the paying passenger could be moved."

"Oooh! No! I couldn't move a gentleman like Master Calvin Cartwright!" Captain Walsh gasped. In the last of the disappearing quayside torch light he squinted closely at our faces. "Did I do something wrong?" he asked.

Chapter Nine

"I will tell truth, by grace itself I swear"

The journey south through the early winter storms would have been unpleasant anyway, but with Calvin Cartwright on board it was a nightmare. He would stand on the afterdeck and preach openly to the crew, or take them aside and whisper his lies in their ears.

Meg and I had sailed on troubled voyages with these men before and they had accepted us as their friends. Now some of them were muttering prayers every time they had to cross our paths. "A woman on board's unlucky," I overheard one say. "But a witch on board is certain death!"

"Maybe she'll vanish overboard one night in a storm."

I stepped forward. "If she does, I'll make sure you are cut into a thousand pieces and fed to the fishes," I said in my most pleasant voice.

The man crossed himself and gave a weak, gap-toothed grin. "Just telling stories of mermaids, Master William," he said and slid away over the deck like the water snake that he was.

"Who are you threatening, William?" my father asked.

"The crew are close to mutiny because they believe Cartwright's story that we are a witch's helpers."

"I see," said my father, stroking his fine beard to a point. "Do these men know a witch from a watchtower?"

"I don't think so, Father."

"Then let's find out, shall we?" He climbed to the after-deck and ordered the sails to be lowered and the anchor dropped for the night. "I want you all in the shelter of the foredeck ... except for a lookout," he told the men. "Where's Cartwright?"

"In his cabin, Sir James."

"Just slip a bolt across his door and make sure he stays there. Now, the rest of you, let's have a talk before supper."

When they gathered, curious, he told them to sit on the deck while he sat on a coil of rope and looked down on them. "There's a lot of talk about witchcraft on this ship. How many of you have met a witch or a wizard?"

The men looked around, but no one answered.

"You are experts on witches yet you've never met one! Strange. Have you even heard of a real witch?"

"Aye! John Dee!" a deck hand cried.

My father looked pleased. "But you never got to meet the famous Doctor Dee?"

"Of course not!"

"Then it may interest you to know that *I* did."

The men looked impressed. "What was he like, Sir James?" someone asked.

"I'm glad you asked me that. If you want to hear a *true* witch story, then I'll tell you one." And Father leaned forward, his forearms on his knees and began his tale …

SIR JAMES MARSDEN'S STORY

You all know that my mother, Lady Eleanor Marsden, was a lady-in-waiting to our good queen and her mother. Now John Dee advised our queen on horoscopes. If a wise man or woman tells your fortune at a fairground, they face a day in the stocks, but if the Queen chooses an astrologer to read her future, it can't be a hanging crime.

Remember that when you are seeking out witches.

And it's no crime to give medicines and ointments for illnesses and injuries. Jane Atkinson has been doing that for years and no one who took her herbs and potions ever accused her of working with the Devil … until that Puritan Cartwright came along! If my son and young Meg Lumley helped her, they did it out of Christian goodness – not out of hellish badness.

I see one or two of you are having second thoughts now. You should be ashamed of yourselves. Calvin Cartwright is a powerful preacher, but that doesn't make him *right*.

But I was going to tell you about Doctor John Dee, wasn't I? My mother told me all about him when I was a young man. He was married and lived in a house at Mortlake near London, and had said to Lady Eleanor that she would be welcome to visit him at any time. He included me in the invitation, although he'd never met me.

I've told you before how I fought under Sir Francis Drake against the Spanish Armada. After we'd sent Philip's ships to the bottom of the ocean – or at least limping back to Spain – I found I had a day to spare in London and decided to visit Doctor Dee.

He has never been popular. When I asked for directions in Mortlake, people shut their doors against me, or spat at me and crossed themselves. One man told me that Dee had had his house wrecked on many occasions while he was away in Europe, selling his magic secrets. But at least the man pointed me in the direction of Dee's house. And a fine house it was too. It had a large garden and great glass windows; there was enough room for half a dozen servants.

One of them answered the door. He had a thin, suspicious face and eyes that never stayed still. He wore a strange black cap that was pulled down to cover his ears. I wondered if he could hear me. "I've come to see Doctor John Dee," I explained.

"Why?" said the man, glaring at me as if I were a figger come to steal the family silver.

"My mother, Lady Eleanor Marsden, was a friend of his at the court of Queen Elizabeth."

"And my mother was the Empress of China," the man said rudely.

"You don't look Chinese," I said.

"What do you want?" he snapped at me.

"To see your master."

"He's busy."

I admit my temper was getting a little short. "Will you be so good as to tell him that James Marsden would like to see him."

"I'm not a servant!" he said fiercely. "Why should I carry your messages?"

I took a step back. It's true I *had* thought he was a servant. "My good sir!" I cried. "I am so very sorry. I thought you were Doctor Dee's steward."

He wiped his dripping nose on the sleeve of his black gown and said, "Steward indeed! I'm Edward Kelley, his guide and scryer."

"His what?" I asked. I was not happy being kept waiting on the doorstep like this with half the street coming out to listen to our conversation.

"Scryer. Doctor Dee has a powerful crystal. It is a window to the spirit world."

"Witchcraft?" I cried.

Edward Kelley's eyes flickered up and down the street to see who'd overheard my cry. He grasped my elbow and dragged me into the house. "The poor doctor has already had his house wrecked by the mob who think he's a witch! He is not! He is a great man. An alchemist, a mathematician and a collector of books."

"But he talks to devils through a magic crystal, you said!"

Kelley looked at me, furious, for a second, then his eyes slid away to the dark corners of the wood-panelled hall. "I said nothing of the sort!" he hissed. Spittle spattered the front of my best velvet doublet. "I *said* he has a powerful crystal. It is inhabited by *angels*, not devils. But Dee cannot speak to the angels himself. That's why he needs me. I'm his scryer. I can see into the crystal and hear the angel voices. I tell him what they say."

It sounded strange but wonderful, and I was about to ask for a demonstration when a voice called, "Who's there, Edward?"

"Someone called Mudsome," the man replied. The cap over his ears must have weakened his hearing.

"Marsden!" I called to the man who was walking down the stairs. He was tall, slightly stooped and with white hair covered by a skullcap. Under his long white beard I could see that his face had once been handsome. This must be the famous Doctor Dee.

"Lady Eleanor's son!" he cried. "Wonderful!" He shook me warmly by the hand and invited me to dinner with his wife, his seven children and Kelley. It was clear that the children were afraid of the black-capped Kelley and Mistress Joan Dee disliked him. We ate the dinner of chicken in garlic sauce in silence.

"My mother has often told me about your skill in reading the future in the stars," I said when we had finished dinner with a rose-flavoured cream dish.

"Ah!" Dee chuckled. "I have something much more powerful now." His wife glared at him, but he went on happily, "My Show Stone!"

"A stone?"

"Well, more of a crystal really. Come up to my room and look at it. If the spirit Madini is free today she may speak to you."

I have to admit I was nervous at getting mixed up with

his sorcery, but I was interested. Wouldn't you be? Dee led the way upstairs to a small room. One wall was lined with books. The window on the other wall was shuttered so the room was almost in darkness, and the only furniture was a table with a bench at either side. On the table stood the Show Stone: a clear crystal that shone even in the gloom.

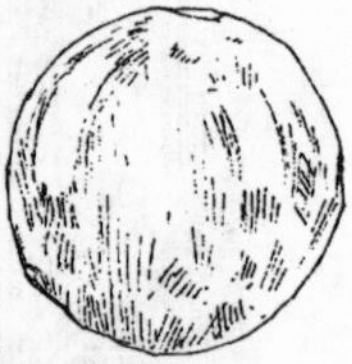

"Edward here will speak to the stone and see if it has any message for us today," Dee said quietly. "Sit next to me."

I sat next to Dee and Kelley sat across the table from us. Kelley stared into the crystal for a long time. In the near-darkness I could see little, but I could smell the dust and the rotting wood of the floor and the leather covers of the books. Then I sensed another, more human smell. The smell of dirty feet.

Suddenly Kelly gave a cry. "Madini is here!" he said. His voice was hoarse. "Take my hands!"

Dee arranged us so that we linked hands in a circle around the crystal. "Why do we need to do this?" I whispered.

"It is a custom. There are cheats and tricksters around in this wicked world. While we hold Master Kelley's hands he cannot try any fraud on us," Dee explained.

Suddenly there was a sharp rap on the table. I felt the table jump up and the shock made my heart stop. Kelley began speaking in his hoarse, low voice. "In the middle of the stone I see a small round spark of fire. See! It's growing! It dazzles me!"

"I see nothing," I murmured to Dee.

"No, but Kelley does!"

"Ah, the light is gone. And now a mist! Ah! See? The mist parts like a curtain! See? The Queen! Ah! The curtain has drawn again." Kelley moaned as if he were in pain.

"What does it mean?" Dee urged.

Kelley shook his head. "We must ask Madini!"

"Who's that?" I asked.

"A spirit girl," Dee said. "She helps Kelley with his scrying."

"Madini!" Kelley called.

There was a great hammering on the wall of the room to my left. The sound echoed and died, leaving me very frightened. "Is that you, Madini?"

There was a single crash of something hammering on the wall. "One rap means 'yes'," Dee explained.

"Have you seen the image of the Queen?"

Crash!

"Can you tell me what it means?"

Crash!

There was silence for a minute. Dee whispered, "Madini will try to talk, but it takes all her energy for days!"

At last a thin, girlish voice came from the direction of the crystal. We fixed our eyes on it. "Visit the Queen," the spirit said. I looked up at Kelley. His mouth was slightly open, but his lips were not moving. Then I caught a whiff of a new scent. Garlic. "Show her the pan," the girl's voice said. Again Kelley's lips didn't move, but the garlic drifted into my nostrils. "Ask her for money." More garlic.

"Money for the magic powder?" Dee asked the Show Stone.

"Yes-s-s!" Enough garlic to make my eyes water.

And I knew who Madini was.

"The spark is gone from the crystal," Kelley sighed.

"Then let us go into my library and look at the pan," Dee said, rubbing his hands together happily while I slipped the drawstring from the purse at my belt and lowered it carefully to the floor beneath the table.

We rose and left the room. Dee's library was filled with books of every size. They were jammed into shelves or lying open on tables or scattered on chairs. Some were

bound in thick leather with gold lettering and others were not much more than a few sheets stitched together. There were other stones like the crystal, perched on the window-sill or on top of the book shelves. One that Dee called his Black Mirror was something I recognized. It was a simple lump of coal, polished till it was mirror bright. "I'd give my whole purse for something as beautiful as that," I lied, and slapped my side. I looked down and said, "The Devil take me! I've lost my purse. I had it at dinner. It must be on the floor of your scrying room, Doctor Dee, I'm sorry."

"I'll get it," Kelley said quickly, his shifting eyes flickering like sunlight on a lake.

But I was ready for him and had my hand on the door. I turned slightly so that my shoulder blocked his path, and was out of the door and down the passage before he could stop me. I reached the room and pulled back the shutters. I was on my hands and knees under the table by the time Kelley reached it. "Have you found it?" he asked.

I felt under the table and pulled out a walking stick with a metal knob on the end. On the floor, under Kelley's chair, there was the mark of a damp footprint. "Yes, and I've found this too," I said, lifting the walking stick.

"I wonder how that got there?" he asked.

"Maybe Madini dropped it," I said, smiling.

I tied my purse back on to my belt and walked past him to the library. Doctor Dee held a metal frying pan in his hand and held it up to the window. "Look at this, Marsden!" he said.

"It's not much use to anyone," I said. The pan had a shape cut from the bottom, a shape rather like the head of a horse.

Dee's eyes sparkled. "It is quite priceless!" he laughed. "My friend Edward cut that shape from the bottom of the pan."

"A bit of a waste," I said, but Kelley looked smug, yet a little watchful.

"He heated up the metal in a crucible," Doctor Dee said eagerly, showing me the crucible on the table. "Then he stirred in a very special powder," he went on, picking up a metal rod and miming the action. "Finally he poured the melted metal back into the hole. I have it here," he said. He was like a child with a new toy. He placed a piece of metal in the bottom of the pan. It fitted perfectly. Then he handed the metal to me to examine.

I knew from the weight and the feel of it that this was pure gold.

"You have discovered the Philosopher's Stone," I said.

"That's right," Dee said. "The stone that men have sought for thousands of years. The stone that turns ordinary metals into gold! It is in the form of powder, of course, not stone."

"Where is this powder?" I asked.

Doctor Dee unlocked a chest that stood on the floor of his library and pulled out two pouches, rather smaller than my purse. He opened the drawstrings carefully, scarcely daring to breathe. I looked into the purses. One held a white powder and the other a red. "Of course," Dee explained, "The powders can't be mixed in the same bag. They would turn the bag to gold!"

"Of course," I said. As I leaned forward my hand rested on the metal stirring-rod. I slipped it into the sleeve of my shirt without Kelley or Dee noticing. Even as my finger pushed it into my sleeve I felt that it was not a rod, but a narrow, hollow tube.

"Now Madini tells me I must take this discovery to Her Majesty Queen Elizabeth. With this we can make England the greatest nation on earth!" Dee smiled happily.

I hadn't the heart to tell him the truth.

"I wish you luck," I said to Doctor Dee, as I fastened my cloak and picked up my hat ready to leave his house. "I'm only sorry I can't stay to see the Queen's joy. I sail back to Durham on this evening's tide. But it has been wonderful to meet you, Doctor, after all my mother has told me about you."

He smiled happily and walked down the stairs with me. Edward Kelley seemed eager to hang at Dee's shoulder so that the doctor and I would have no time alone together, but Doctor Dee turned to him and said, "Prepare my writing implements, Edward. I will write to the Queen at once. After her great victory over the Spanish Armada this news will fill her with joy as pure as our gold."

Kelley looked uncertain. His eyes began to flicker again. Silently and sullenly he began to climb the stairs. At the front door of the house I turned to Doctor Dee and said, "Where did Kelley get the Philosopher's Stone?"

"From the most mystical and ancient site in the whole of Britain. From near the tomb of the fabulous King Arthur himself. From Glastonbury Abbey! He was told where to find it in a dream. Isn't it wonderful?"

"My mother admired and liked you, Doctor Dee. And for that love I want you to promise me one thing," I said carefully.

"What's that?"

"Do not take the stone to the Queen until you have tried it for yourself – wait until Kelley is out of the city. Will you do that?"

The happiness faded from his eyes. "Edward has been a rogue in the past. But I need him as a scryer. Do you think he is deceiving me over the gold?"

"Just try it when Kelley is not present."

He frowned, then nodded slowly. "What you say is sensible." He looked at me with a steady gaze. "You're as wise as your mother. Give her my love and my best wishes," he said and closed the door.

I came back home to Durham and the Marsden estate, but always asked travellers for news from London. And, do you know, I never heard of Elizabeth suddenly becoming rich because of the magic of the Philosopher's Stone.

I wonder why that should be?

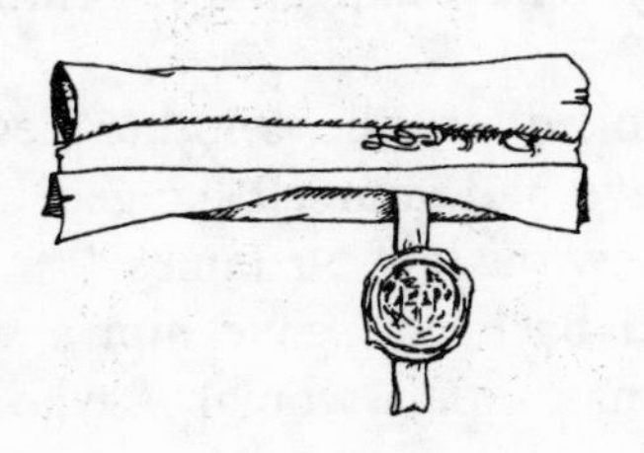

Chapter Ten

"You are a vagabond and no true traveller"

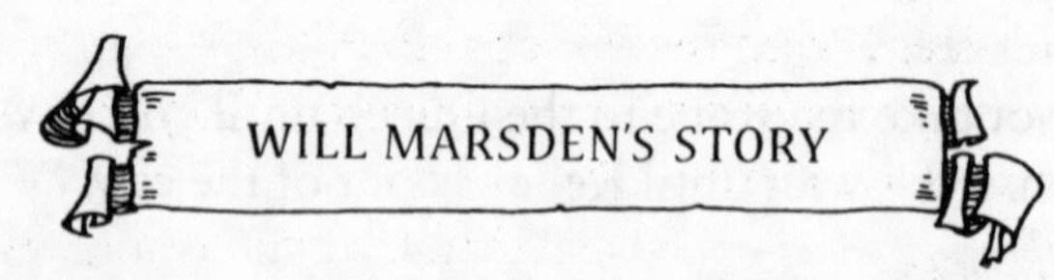

My father sat on the coil of rope looking pleased with himself. The crew had been fascinated by the story. Now he turned to them and asked, "What would you have done with Dee?"

"Hanged him!" the first mate growled.

"Why?" enquired my father.

The sailor looked surprised at the question. "Why ... you saw him talking with the Devil."

"But he said it was an angel."

"The Devil often says he's an angel just to trap people," a deck hand said.

"Would you have hanged Edward Kelley too?"

"Of course!"

"And would you have hanged me?" Father asked. "After all, I was there."

The men looked at one another, less certain now. "Would *you* have had yourself hanged?" Captain Walsh asked. "You know the law, Sir James."

Father leaned back and gave him a wintry smile. "I would hang a man – or a woman – who talked with the

Devil. I would hang Jane Atkinson and I would hang my own son if I thought they were guilty. But John Dee hadn't talked to the Devil!"

"You said he did!" the first mate objected angrily. "You told us you heard the Devil rap on the table and on the wall. You heard him speak in the voice of Madini!"

"I told you I smelled the stink of feet and a whiff of garlic," my father said quietly. "I told you what I found on the floor under the table." He was enjoying some joke of his own, but I couldn't see what it was.

"Stop tormenting the crew, Sir James," Meg Lumley said. "Tell them what really happened!"

My father pretended to be indignant. "They can work it out for themselves! After all, I did!"

Meg shook her head, walked across to the coil of rope and sat down next to him. "Edward Kelley was a fake. He could no more speak to spirits than I could fly a broomstick."

"There's some people say you *can* do that, Miss Meg!" Captain Walsh called and the crew laughed. The mood was changing and the men were showing less fear and hatred towards us.

Meg gave a pained smile. "Sir James smelled stinking feet. If Edward Kelley had washed them, he might never have been discovered. As soon as they sat at the table, Kelley had slipped off one of his boots – maybe both of them. You've seen acrobats at the fairs and markets. They can use their toes like fingers. They train themselves. That's what Kelly did. He picked up the stick with his feet, rapped under the table top, then stretched out a leg and rapped on the wall."

The men nodded. "It's easy when you know how it's done," said the first mate.

"What about Madini's voice?" I asked.

"Easy," Meg said. "I've watched actors do it on stage. They speak through their teeth and keep their lips and jaws still." She slipped a piece of coal from her pocket. It was as smooth as a mirror on one side. She looked into it. "Tell me, magic mirror, do you think I'm a witch?"

We all stared hard at the coal and a thin voice replied, "No. It's all a trick!"

Of course, it was Meg's voice from the back of her throat. The men laughed and one asked, "How do you know that's what Kelley did?"

"Because I can freeze my lips, but I have to use my breath. Every time the spirit spoke Sir James smelled garlic. Do they eat garlic in the spirit world?"

"No!" the first mate cried. "But Kelley and Dee had been eating chicken in garlic sauce for dinner!"

"Exactly!" Meg said.

"Yes," I said, "that explains *how* Kelley tricked Dee, but it doesn't explain *why*. What did he hope to gain?"

Meg frowned. "Money, I guess. Dee wouldn't go to the Queen with the Philosopher's Stone – unless a spirit voice ordered him to. He didn't trust Kelley enough to do it at Kelley's suggestion. The Queen would pay Kelley a fortune to get her hands on those red and white powders. Once Kelley had her money, he would disappear with it."

"No!" Captain Walsh said. "That doesn't make sense. He could make all the gold he wanted just using the powders. Why would he want the Queen's gold?"

I was beginning to see the plot. "Making gold from a piece of frying pan must have been a trick too – but I can't see how he could manage it."

The crew shook their heads and muttered among themselves. Finally I called to Meg, "Tell us how Kelley made gold from iron. You're just bursting to show your cleverness."

Meg poked out her tongue at me and said, "Sir James gave you the clue. He was clever enough to see it. Why can't you?"

"Oh, get on with it," I groaned. "Tell us!"

"Kelley set up a crucible and heated it over the fire. He cut a piece from the bottom of the pan and pretended to drop it into the crucible. He probably slipped it into his pocket. Then he sprinkled a pinch of the powders into the crucible and stirred it with the rod. But the rod was hollow. It was packed with gold dust and had a plug of wax in the end. When the rod went in the crucible, the wax plug melted and the gold dust ran into the crucible. The gold melted and Kelly poured it out. Dee saw a scrap of metal go in and gold come out – he was sure that the powder had made the change!"

"Ah, but what's the good of that?" the first mate asked. "It would cost Kelley a few pounds to get the gold dust – and all he'd have left at the end would be a lump of gold worth the same amount."

"No!" cried Meg. "If he spent five pounds on the gold, it

was money well spent. He could sell his magic powder for twenty pounds or more to the greedy fools who saw the performance. The Queen might have paid him a thousand!"

The crew nodded again. "But Dee never took it to the Queen?" the first mate asked.

"Not after I'd had a word with him," Father said. "He went on telling her horoscope and she went on supporting some of his experiments, but he must have followed my advice and not tried to sell her the Philosopher's Stone. I suppose he must be dead by now. He'd be seventy-five-years old if he lived."

"And what happened to Edward Kelley?" a deck hand asked.

"He got what he deserved in the end. He was caught out with his trickery and arrested in the city of Prague. He tried to climb over a wall to escape one night. But the drop was greater than he thought and he broke both his legs and burst something in his guts. He died seven years ago."

The men on the deck nodded, satisfied. My father leaned forward. "So, you see, there was no *witchcraft* ... just *trickery*. Dee was a fool and Kelley was a villain. But would you have hanged them?"

"No," the men muttered.

"So why are you so keen to hang me and Will Marsden?" Meg asked. "Nobody's talked to a devil ... though there has been some trickery going on in the graveyard at Marsden. The witnesses in Jane's trial were fools and the people who put them up to it were villains. But Jane's not a witch, and neither am I."

The first mate rose to his feet. He looked awkward, but was brave enough to say, "Some of us got it wrong, Miss Meg. I'm sorry."

There were mumbles of agreement.

My father cleared his throat and looked as uncomfortable as the first mate. "As our friend Calvin Cartwright

would tell you, greed is a terrible thing. It makes you blind to simple tricks." He took the piece of coal from Meg's hand. "My greed for the black gold cost me a great deal and it started all these witchcraft problems for a harmless old woman. I hope it's not too late to put things right." My father turned to Captain Walsh. "It's time we let this good crew have their dinner."

"Aye, Sir James," Walsh said, as the men stirred themselves.

Meg turned to my father and rested her hand on his arm. "That was a brilliant story, Sir James. It'll make the rest of the journey a lot more pleasant for Will and me."

"Thank you, Meg," he said. "I hope so. Of course, our troubles really start when we get to London."

"When will that be?" I asked.

"Tomorrow evening if the wind stays in this south-west corner," he said. My father was a good sailor and he was right as usual.

When we reached the mouth of the Thames, the crew took to the ship's boat and towed us upriver towards the setting sun. They rowed through the stench of human waste and the rubbish that poured into the old river. Even on deck the smell was choking and mixed with the sooty smoke of thousands of coal fires. Black flakes spotted our white collars and tasted bitter in our mouths. The coal burned in London would make the Marsden family a fortune, but it blotted out the evening sky and turned the falling sun a bloody red.

When we landed, the shadows were long and the alleys as dark as a Durham mine. It was time for the rats to run through those dark passages between the shops and houses and taverns. The harmless rats had four legs – the really dangerous ones ran on two and carried daggers.

Calvin Cartwright was the first man to march down the gangplank and disappear into the city without a backward glance. My father sighed. "London is ruled by the council and the council is full of his Puritan brothers," he explained, as he watched Cartwright go.

From our berth on the quayside I could see the towering shape of the Globe Theatre where I'd start rehearsals the next day. "The Puritans hate the theatre," I said. "They try to close it down at the slightest excuse. A violent play or a fight in the theatre. It's only Queen Elizabeth's love of plays that keeps us going. She defends us against the Puritans. The theatre people are worried about what'll happen when she dies."

My father leaned on the rail and peered into the fading light. "Not just the theatre people, Will. I think everyone's worried."

"Well," Meg said cheerfully, "if this is the last season of plays, you'd better make the most of it!"

Lanterns and torches lit some of the windows in the darkening city. My father looked at them and said, "You two are like the city there. Will looks at it and sees only the darkness. Meg looks at it and sees only the light."

"So who's right?" I asked, surprised at his wisdom.

"Both of you … neither of you," he said. "You need each other – one to see the path ahead and the other to see the traps. Together you'll save Jane Atkinson."

"And you?" I asked.

"I'll work with my friend Sir Robert Carey to beat the Puritans in the law courts. But it's no use winning back Widow Atkinson's land if she loses her life, is it? You have to find a way to the Queen and get a pardon. That's the only thing that'll stop Calvin Cartwright."

"The Queen is dying," I said … and I realized I was looking at the dark side, just as Father said I did.

"Then we'd better hurry," Meg said … looking at the light.

Chapter Eleven

"What hath been cannot be"

We spent the night on the ship because it was safer than lodging in some strange, flea-ridden London tavern. I stayed awake most of the night, learning my part in Master Shakespeare's *All's Well that Ends Well*. The excitement of joining the actors would have kept me awake anyway, but I was word-perfect by the time I walked down the gang-plank with Meg. It's strange that I never got to speak those words on stage.

The Globe Theatre was a short walk from the quay. There was a light rain falling. Not enough to flush the filth from the streets, but enough to make it a gloomy day. "It can only get better," Meg said cheerfully.

For once she was wrong. It got worse. We could see there was something wrong at the Globe as soon as we turned the corner into Maiden Lane. I could make out the high forehead and great dark eyes of the playwright, William Shakespeare. He was standing at the entrance to the theatre and waving his hands at the group of men in black cloaks and hats who surrounded him.

"Puritans," Meg said.

We lengthened our strides to get there quicker and see what was going on. A grey-haired Puritan seemed to be the leader of the group and he was roaring at Master Shakespeare as if he were in church, delivering a sermon. "You are sinners, all of you! We all know that sin causes the plague!"

His friends cheered in agreement. Actors and stage-hands came out of the Globe and stood behind Master Shakespeare.

"Plays cause sin, so plays cause the plague!" the Puritan shouted.

The playwright wiped the damp from his forehead with a weary hand. "We have a licence to perform, councillor."

"Where is it?"

Master Shakespeare looked unhappy. "It is being brought from the Queen by one of her officers this morning."

"Until we see this so-called licence I order that this theatre be closed."

"We aren't open!" a stagehand called. "We're just re-hearsing. We open next week."

"Not for long," a short red-faced Puritan sneered. "We need just one excuse to close this theatre and cancel your licence."

"Yes!" another added. "Just one fight or complaint of a disturbance."

"Or a robbery!" the grey-haired leader nodded. "There's not a sinful performance goes by without a robbery taking place. Those crowds of people are a swamp where the pick-pocket toads breed."

"And your evil entertainments prevent people from going to church. As a result they go straight to Hell when they die!"

"I thought the Puritans believed we all go to Hell anyway," Master Shakespeare answered.

"The chosen ones go to heaven – but they miss that glorious chance if they are tempted into your pit of misery," the fat Puritan pointed out.

The playwright spread his hands. "Gentlemen, we are breaking no laws. You cannot close the theatre unless we do."

"You are wrong," a Puritan at the back of the group said. He had been turned away from me and his collar was raised against the rain, so I hadn't seen his face. But he had seen mine. Now he turned, swept an arm towards us and pointed. The straight eyebrows and the angled face showed some triumph. "You are employing one of Satan's servants!"

The Puritans all turned to look at me. Some were shocked, some afraid and some curious. "What? Will Marsden?" Master Shakespeare said, looking across at me. "He's an honest, church going lad."

Calvin Cartwright drew himself up to his full height and looked down his fine nose. "That boy is under suspicion of witchcraft!"

His words caused an uproar amongst the councillors and some of them clasped their hands and started muttering prayers. Master Shakespeare walked across to me and wrapped an arm around my shoulders to show his support for me. "Is this true, Will?"

"Yes. Cartwright's friends have accused me. But I am innocent," I said.

"You are guilty until you have proved yourself innocent!" Cartwright boomed and the Puritan councillors cheered him. "This theatre must close at once."

"We have a licence from the Queen – or we soon will have," an actor tried to argue.

"The Queen will take away your licence as soon as she

hears you are employing a witch," the grey-haired Puritan said, to more loud cheers.

"There's no such thing," Meg cried and the yells died suddenly.

Calvin Cartwright turned on her. "The Bible says there are witches. Are you saying the Bible is wrong?" he asked.

It was a clever trap. If Meg said the Bible was false, she'd be arrested as a heretic – if she said it was true, she was agreeing there were such things as witches. She chewed her lip and said, "No."

"Then the theatre closes!" the fat Puritan thundered.

I felt the weight of Master Shakespeare's arm across my shoulders as he slumped in defeat. Not even his great wit could conquer these men. There was only one door that led out of the problem and I held the key. I stepped forward. "I am not joining Master Shakespeare's company," I said. "I just came to tell him that my father needs my help with his business in London." I looked into Master Shakespeare's sad eyes. "I won't be acting in this play, sir."

He was unhappy and confused. I knew what he was feeling. He didn't want to give in to these bullies, yet he didn't want to abandon the play he'd spent so much time writing. The actors too were desperate to make some money after the theatre had been closed by the plague. Some had been selling their costumes to feed themselves through the autumn. Closing the theatre would be a disaster.

"Will, you can't let them tell these lies about you," he said.

Meg came to my help. "It won't be for long, Master Shakespeare. We'll clear our names and be back for your next play, I promise."

He looked at her and said, "You'll look after him, will you?"

"Of course," she said brightly. "I may have to crack a few Puritan heads together, but we'll get through this."

The playwright looked relieved. I felt miserable, but tried to use my acting skills to look happy for him. "Back to work!" the playwright called.

"Not until you have a licence!" the Puritan leader said sternly.

Master Shakespeare looked up as a horseman rode down Maiden Lane towards the Globe. "I think you'll find this is Her Majesty's officer now."

The man on the horse was dressed in dark, rich velvet, but his fine appearance was spoiled by a ruff that sagged as the starch was soaked in the rain. He was a handsome man of about forty with a neat brown beard and a fresh and friendly face.

He jumped lightly to the ground and walked with slightly bowed legs towards the Puritans. "Good day, alderman!" he said to the leading councillor.

"God be with you, Master Carey," the Puritan said sourly.

"Here's the licence," the officer said with a grin. "I'll bet you are pleased to see it, eh? You must have been worried, weren't you?"

The alderman glared at the Queen's messenger, glanced at the document, then thrust it at Master Shakespeare. "One fight, one robber, one disturbance, and that licence is worthless," he said, before turning on his heel and leading the black-cloaked men away. Calvin Cartwright lingered long enough to give Meg and me a cold stare. "I'll see your bodies burn on this earth before your spirits burn in Hell," he said.

"If we were witches we'd hang," Meg said quietly.

"Perhaps the Scottish King will bring his Scottish laws with him," Cartwright said. "I hope the old woman dies soon and the law lets me burn you," he went on. "Kings know how to treat sinners better than any queen would."

"Are you saying Queen Elizabeth is a bad queen?" Meg asked.

Cartwright knew better than to say that, especially with Master Carey, her officer, looking on. "The Bible says all the wickedness in the world is nothing compared to the wickedness of a woman."

"Does that include your mother?" Meg asked.

Cartwright took a quick step forward and raised his hand to strike her, as Master Shakespeare and I cried, "No!"

Carey was a man of action. He stepped between Cartwright and Meg and smiled. "I cannot let you strike a lady," he said calmly.

"Lady?"

"If you strike her I will challenge you to a duel," he said and slipped the glove off his right hand, ready to slap it across Cartwright's hard face.

Cartwright stepped back. "When King James takes the old woman's throne, he will deal with you too," he threatened.

"I look forward to that," Carey grinned, and watched Cartwright stalk down the street, splashing through the grey puddles. He surprised Meg by taking her hand and kissing it. She surprised me by blushing.

"Thanks for that, Sir Robert," William Shakespeare

said. "And thanks to you, Will Marsden, for stepping aside from this production. I'll make sure you have a wonderful part in my next one. Come and see *All's Well that Ends Well* when we perform it. Goodbye for now, Meg. Take care of yourself."

He tucked his precious licence under his doublet to protect it from the rain and walked back into the Globe.

Carey looked at me carefully. "Marsden?" he said. "There's a Marsden family that lives in the north. Are you related to them?"

"We live in County Durham," I said.

"And is your grandfather Sir Clifford Marsden?" he asked.

"Yes," I said. "You know him?"

"A wonderful man! Your father must be Sir James, is that right?"

"He is."

"We served together against the Spanish Armada back in 1588. Give him my best wishes. Tell him Robert Carey was asking after his health."

"Tell him yourself," Meg grinned. "He's just five minutes away, looking after the unloading of his ship."

"Marvellous! Wonderful!" Sir Robert Carey cried. "It's almost dinner time. Perhaps we can all dine together and you can tell me the news from the north."

Before we had a chance to turn down the invitation, he had taken the bridle of his fine bay horse and begun leading it towards the docks. He talked very fast, asked a thousand questions and sometimes didn't wait for an answer.

"Your grandfather was a legend on the Scottish Borders. A great fighter and a respected captain. He served Sir John Forster, didn't he? Well, I took over Sir John's command when he became too old. It was a wonderful life! Hunting down Scottish cattle thieves, chasing them through the hills back to their pitiful homes. Watching a dozen of the villains hanging from the same gallows tree at times."

"We don't like to think about gallows," Meg said.

"Sorry! Sorry! I forgot. That Puritan was saying something about a witchcraft charge against you. Is that right?" he asked.

"We were hoping to get a pardon if we came to London," I said.

"Got any money?" Carey asked suddenly.

"Why?"

"Because in Queen Elizabeth's court you can buy anything. The court is like a huge clock with a thousand wheels and cogs. Money is the grease that keeps them running smoothly."

"I haven't much," I admitted.

"Never mind. Perhaps your father can help."

"He has his own problems," I said, and explained about the fight for Jane Atkinson's corner of Bournmoor Woods.

"We'll soon sort that out!" Carey laughed. "It's just as well you met me," he said, and strode ahead. Meg and I were half running to keep up with him.

"That's our ship, the *Hawk*," I said, pointing to the collier that was having its load of coal shovelled into waiting carts.

"Sir James!" Carey cried, when he saw my father on the foredeck.

My father walked down stiffly to meet the officer and began to bow. But Carey just slapped him on the back. "James! It's good to see you again. I've just met your fine son and daughter."

My father looked as though he'd swallowed a wasp. "Meg Lumley is my wife's maidservant," he said.

"Ah! Sorry, young Meg. Easy mistake to make. You look like the daughter of a great family like the Marsdens." He turned back to my father. "How much money do you have, James?"

"What?" my father said, blinking.

"Money. I can solve your problems if you can line a few purses on the way. You need an early hearing in the Star Chamber if you're going to defeat those Puritans – but the good news is the Queen hates the Puritans and her judges know it. A couple of hundred pounds should do it."

"Two hundred pounds?" my father said weakly.

"Plus fifty for my own time and service. I'd normally ask for a hundred, but since you're the son of Sir Clifford and we are old shipmates, I'll do it for half. How is the old man, by the way?"

"Well enough, when we left Wearmouth."

"And Lady Eleanor?"

"She had a heavy cold, but a woman herbalist from the village was caring for her."

"Good, good," Carey said. He turned to a coal carter and said, "Here's a groat. Take my horse on the ship and find it some oats. I'm off to a tavern with Sir James."

The man's energy was leaving us breathless and my father dazed. "The Mermaid is a good enough tavern. Just don't order the fish. A couple of my friends were as sick as cats last week."

We began to walk back over the quay towards the tangle

of narrow alleys. They were dirtier than the main streets, but there was less chance of being crushed under the wheels of a cart or trodden on by a horse. "Can you just buy a pardon for us?" Meg asked.

"Not quite so simple. That'll have to come from the Queen herself. It would be best if young Will here could ask in person."

"Me? Talk to the Queen?"

"Why not? She likes a good-looking young man. Hah! How do you think I got on so well? It wasn't for my brains, I can tell you. The Queen's my cousin, but that wouldn't win me any favours. No, it's a matter of knowing how to keep the old crow sweet."

"But I can't just walk up to the palace and ask to see the Queen," I objected.

"You *can* just walk up and ask," Carey said, turning into the low doorway of a tavern that smelled of tobacco smoke and stale beer. "The trouble is you would never get to see her," he added, pushing his way through to a table by the window. He took off his hat and shook the rain from it. "A flagon of wine!" he called to a serving girl in a grubby apron over an even dirtier blue dress. "And what's to eat?"

"Oyster stew, sir, or veal pastries."

"Let's have a large veal pastry – enough for four hungry people," Carey said.

My father squeezed himself into a space on the bench between two men in leather aprons who stank of fish.

"If I can't get to see the Queen, what's the point in going?" I asked.

"Grease, young Will. Plenty of grease. A hundred pounds should buy your way to the head of the queue – and of course the Queen likes a gift. Say another hundred."

"Two hundred pounds?" my father said. In the weak light of the window his face was as grey as the Thames.

"Plus the usual fifty for me," Carey added.

"So, all I have to do is give you five hundred pounds and you will solve all our problems?" my father said.

The two men – they must have been fishmongers – looked at him as if he were one of the mermaids from the inn sign come to life. Five hundred pounds was more than they'd earn in their lives.

"That's about it, my old friend," Carey said, and took the wine flagon from the serving girl. He began to fill the four goblets from her tray. "Living at court is an expensive business, James. The Queen wants gifts and jewels and money from everyone around her. Of course I'd love to help you for nothing, but that's not the way the Queen's court works. So, what's it to be? Are you in or are you out?"

Meg, Carey and I looked at my father. Even the fishmongers had stopped drinking. My father took a deep breath and drew himself up straight. "What's five hundred pounds?" he asked boldly. "I'll get that for the coal that's being unloaded now. Carey, my friend, I think we will accept your offer."

He raised his goblet and touched it lightly against Sir Robert Carey's.

And it had been decided. I was to meet the last of the Tudor monarchs. The fearful Elizabeth herself.

Chapter Twelve

"Take this purse of gold, and let me buy your friendly help"

It took us over a month – and a lot more money – to get me ready for my visit to Whitehall Palace. Robert Carey took me to his own tailor in the Strand and had two suits made for me at ten pounds each, and he began to teach me how to behave when I met the Queen.

"She's a terrifying woman," he said one evening in the Mermaid Tavern where I was lodging. My father had taken *Hawk* back to Wearmouth for another load of coal.

"I thought she liked young men," Meg said. She had taken a job at the tavern so she'd be the link between my father and me when he returned. That evening she sat down with me to hear about the Queen.

"The Queen has always had her own way. She rules by terror. People who disobey – and even people who obey – end up in the Tower! Back in 1587 she ordered Davison, her secretary, to bring her the warrant for Mary Queen of Scots's execution. She signed it and told him to deliver it. Then, when Mary had been beheaded, she said she never meant Mary to lose her head and that Davison was to blame. He was thrown in the Tower and given a heavy fine."

"So, I have to do exactly what the Queen tells me," I said.

Carey threw back his head and laughed. "Lord, no! The Queen hates toadies. She likes a man who stands up to her. That's why she likes me! She likes my sense of adventure. She still remembers the time I walked from London to Berwick to win a two-thousand-pound bet! Oh, yes, she's banned me from court in my time, but I'm back in favour now."

"Why did she ban you?" Meg asked.

"For the same reason she's banned so many." He leaned forward as if he were about to tell us a great secret. "The Queen thinks every man who sees her loves her – and, of course, we all pretend we do! She gets very angry when one of her gentlemen at court gets married. So we do it without telling her, then she finds out and gets furious. She's been doing it for fifty years! The great Sir Walter Raleigh was her favourite for ten years. When he married his Bess, the Queen had him thrown in the Tower of London. She was just as angry with her old favourite Robert Dudley when she found out he had married Lettice Knollys and with her last favourite, Essex, when he married Frances Walsingham."

"Essex tried to lead a rebellion against her, didn't he?" Meg asked.

"Of course he did. Her jealousy had ruined him. She's a vicious old woman."

"So, you're not married," I said.

"I am! And the Queen was as angry as ever. Of course I was living and fighting on the Borders for Her Majesty, so she couldn't have me thrown in the Tower. She tried to do something just as cruel. She sent me with secret messages to King James in Scotland, but wouldn't give me a passport, so that if I'd been caught by the Scots I'd have been murdered!"

"So what did you do?" I asked.

He sipped his wine and turned his bright eyes on me. "The question is, young Will, what would *you* have done?"

"I'd have had to go," I said.

Carey slapped his forehead with the palm of his hand. "What have I told you?"

"Stand up to her," Meg said.

"Exactly!" he cried. "I refused to go without a passport."

"Didn't she have you arrested for refusing her order?" I asked.

"No. She signed me a passport. I had won. I took messages to King James, but he's as difficult to work with as Queen Elizabeth. He refused to put his answer in writing. He made me remember the message and take it to her. I rode all the way from Edinburgh to find her in Hampton Court. I was covered in mud from the ride. All her lords and ladies were dancing, but I insisted on seeing her in private to give her the King's secret message."

"I thought she'd banned you," I said.

"She had. I spent two hours, on my knees, being screamed at by Her Majesty. I told her I was her most devoted servant and it was her fault I'd married – I said that if she'd been kinder to me I'd never have done it. She liked that! A bit of boldness in her men at court. In the end I kissed her hand and she forgave me. Now I'm the one who's by her side all the time. I'm her favourite."

"Your fortune is made," Meg said.

"It's not!" Sir Robert said. "It costs me all the money I have to stay at court, to keep the Queen happy with rich gifts. Why I even have to play at cards and lose twenty pounds a month. She hates to be beaten, so I have to make sure she never is."

"So why do it if you'd be better off back in Northumberland?" she demanded.

"Because I have a plan that's so bold it will make me my fortune. An idea so simple I daren't even tell you or you might steal it."

"When will you carry out this idea and make your fortune?" I asked.

"When the Queen dies. That's what the whole country is waiting for. The old ways will die with her. It'll be like a springtime for the country when all the brave new buds will burst through." He looked at the window where hail was rattling against the shutters. "Remember, Will, winter doesn't last forever – and neither will the Queen." He slapped my shoulder. "I can't tell you my great plan, but I'll give you a clue. If I were a horse you should put your bets on me. I'll outrun them all and win a great prize."

I shook my head. If it was a riddle I didn't understand it.

"I have to survive the monstrous queen first," I said.

I was worried. If I was too bold she'd have me thrown in the Tower – if I wasn't bold enough she'd just ignore me. Meg saw my fear. "Look at Sir Robert," she said.

"Why?"

"You're an actor, Will. Copy the way Sir Robert behaves and you'll survive," she said. "There's nothing to worry about."

"Just losing my head on the block," I muttered.

Meg grinned. "Then you'll have no worries at all – unless you believe the Puritans and end up in Hell, of course."

Just when I needed sympathy, Meg poked fun at me.

Over the weeks that we waited for the call to go to court we lived in the Mermaid. Every fortnight my father called in with news from Marsden Manor. Calvin Cartwright had returned and was pressing for Widow Atkinson to be brought to trial at the Easter assizes. If she were found guilty, then we'd be brought back from London to follow her to the gallows.

And all of Jane Atkinson's herbs and potions were failing to help my grandmother. She was too weak to leave her bed and Grandfather never left her side.

"They are so spiteful to one another. I always imagined they hated one another," I said.

"They enjoy teasing," Meg said wisely. "If anything happened to your grandmother Sir Clifford would be destroyed."

Christmas came in with bitter northerly winds. I gave Meg a silver locket I'd bought from a craftsman in the city. She gave me her polished coal. She had spent hours with a needle engraving a picture of Marsden Hall on the glass-smooth side. "It's beautiful," I said. She blushed and clutched at the locket around her neck. I'd never seen her lost for words before.

New Year passed and I spent my days wandering the streets of London. I visited the Globe when I could and paid my penny to stand with the groundlings to watch Master Shakespeare's plays. I couldn't bear to watch *All's Well that Ends Well*. I didn't want to see another boy play the part I'd learned. I should have been there on the stage. This witchcraft charge was weighing me down and the waiting was pure misery.

The January snows swept through the streets and covered the filth for a while. London was almost a beautiful city, but the crow-pecked heads of traitors that hung over London Bridge reminded me of death.

Sir Robert Carey visited us with news from the court. The Queen had moved to Richmond Palace because an astrologer had told her that, according to the stars, it was healthier than Whitehall. "So she still believes in the magic of the stars?" I asked.

"She believes in anything her astrologer tells her because he has been with her through the whole of her reign. There are times when I thought all England was ruled on Doctor Dee's advice."

"Dee!" Meg cried, as she entered the room with coal for the blazing tavern fire. "Is he still alive?"

"Yes," Sir Robert said. "A miserable black beetle of a man. He is in charge of a university in a northern town called Manchester. He doesn't get on too well with the Puritans who teach in the college. He visits the Queen whenever he gets the chance. And she needs him now for his witchcraft and his alchemy."

"To make gold?" I asked.

"No, to make medicines. She had a cold last week, but insisted on going out in the snow to show herself to the people outside the palace. Dee says he can cure her, so he's found himself a cosy nest in Richmond for the winter."

"Is the Queen too ill to see people like me?" I asked. I couldn't bear to think of all the time and money I'd wasted.

"Quite the opposite, young Will. She wants to show the world that she is as healthy as ever. She is seeing as many people as she can so they will spread the word that she is fit and well. I'll call for you on Friday and take you to Richmond Palace. I think your time has come, Will."

The river was swollen with melting snow and it was too dangerous to take a boat to Richmond. Sir Robert brought a horse so we could ride the dozen miles to the palace. I had always thought Marsden Hall was large, but it would have fitted into one of the great courtyards of the huge palace by the river. Some of the towers were five stories high and the windows had more glass than Durham Cathedral.

People crowded the slush- and mud-filled roads. An endless stream of carts brought in fresh meat and live animals while carriages carried the rich in and out. There were dozens of horses with riders wrapped against the bitter wind from the icy river while the poor stood around in huddles and palace servants marched through the gateways looking self-important.

Sir Robert rode to a side gate that led into a stable yard, leaped down with his usual energy and handed the reins to a stable boy. "The Queen's been asking for you," the boy said, wiping a huge drip off the end of his nose with the back of his grubby hand.

"When the Queen commands, her humble servants hasten to obey!" Carey said and took long strides over the stable yard to a door set in a tower. "Come up to my rooms, Will, and warm yourself. I'll change out of these boots and riding breeches."

He led the way up a stairway that was well lit by the huge windows. The higher we climbed the better the view I had of the scene below. "It's like a small town!" I said, as I panted to keep up with the Queen's favourite.

His apartments were warm, with fires burning in every room and a troop of servants to keep them fed with coal. His manservant had clothes ready for him and a maid was given the task of showing me Sir Robert's apartments and taking me to my room.

After I'd washed and changed into one of my new suits I found my way into the library where I looked at some of the books. Sir Robert had told me he wasn't much of a scholar, but the books were old and appeared to have been well read. There seemed to be a lot on astronomy and maths. There were some even older ones in Latin that I realized were books on magic.

I turned the pages and read them with wonder. There were instructions on flying. The writer said that a broomstick should be covered in an ointment made from the poison in the wolfsbane plant, boiled with the leaves of the poplar tree, mixed with soot and made into an ointment using human fat. I shuddered at the thought of where the witches would get the human fat.

To see spirits, the book said, you must mix the gall from a bull's liver with crushed ants and the fat of a white hen. There were recipes using blood and the fat of night birds or even baby fat. I could understand why witches were thought to be dangerous – real witches. The ones who meddled with spells and potions like this.

I was so interested in the book I didn't hear the door open.

"The books belong to Doctor Dee," a voice said from the doorway.

I turned to see a woman about my mother's age standing there. She had a plain but pleasant face, and a dress of dark red velvet with embroidered roses in silver thread and a small ruff. "I'm sorry," I said, worried at being caught reading a book on witchcraft. "I'm William Marsden from Durham," I went on, stumbling to my feet.

"I know," said the woman and smiled pleasantly. "I'm Robert's sister."

She held out a hand and I took it and bowed. "I'm honoured."

"My name's Philadelphia, Lady Scrope, but Robert calls me Phil as a pet name. The Queen has her own names for

everyone – and some of them aren't too kind! Her very serious and respectable Secretary of State, Robert Cecil, she calls "Pygmy" – he hates it."

Philadelphia Scrope had bright blue eyes that were as lively as her brother's grey ones, and dark hair that was mostly hidden under a cap. "What does she call you?" I asked.

She pulled her mouth down in a show of mock misery, "'Magpie', because my hair is black, my skin is white and I chatter a lot. But chatterers find out lots of interesting things that dumb swans never learn."

"Have you learned your brother's great secret, the one that is going to make his fortune?" I asked.

"Learned it? I *thought* of it! Oh, I know it's cruel making plans for after the old woman's death, but it's the Queen's own way of life. Grasp your chance while you can. If she wasn't so greedy herself, we wouldn't be as penniless as we are." She nodded towards the book on the table. "Old Dee has nowhere to keep his books in the palace so we charge him to look after them. He grumbles, but Robert just threatens to show them to people in the streets. They have already attacked Dee's house and destroyed his alchemy equipment and torn apart hundreds of his priceless books. If they saw some of these they'd probably tear him apart. They are quite disgusting!"

"Do you think he really is a witch?" I asked her.

"If he is, it's not my place to say. The Queen protects him. All of England wants her dead except John Dee. There's no telling what King James will do when he takes over the throne."

"Do you think he will?"

Philadelphia smiled. "The Queen has refused for forty years to name the person who will take her throne. So some people have been making plans for James to be the next king. Of course the Queen doesn't know, but she must guess that James has friends in her court."

It sounded dangerously close to treason to me. The punishment would be to have a head spiked over London Bridge for the enjoyment of the crows. "Who are those friends?" I asked.

She looked at me carefully. "I'm sure you can keep a secret, Will Marsden. But if you stay here a few days you'll find out soon enough. Everyone in Richmond knows. 'Pygmy' Cecil himself has been writing to King James ... and the messages have been carried by my brother, Robert."

The warm room seemed less comfortable now. With witchcraft books on the shelves and traitors living in the rooms I felt my head slipping into a noose. Philadelphia looked at me and said, "The rewards in this life go to the brave. Be bold, Will Marsden."

"I'll try," I promised. But I wasn't quite prepared to be so bold so soon.

The door was flung open and Robert Carey swept in like a North Sea wind. "The old crow's in a foul mood. She's moaning, 'I'm not well, Robert. I can't sleep.' I told her it's no wonder she can't sleep if she refuses to go to bed! She just says she's afraid that if she goes to bed she'll never get up again!"

"She may be right," his sister said.

"She's up to some plotting with that black beetle John Dee. Perhaps he'll poison her and save us all the trouble," he cried.

I remembered the man who'd had his ears cut off for saying the Queen had plotted Amy Robsart's death. I wondered what the punishment was for plotting Queen Elizabeth's own death. Sir Robert turned to me and gripped my shoulder. "She demanded to know where I'd been when she wanted me to entertain her. I told her about you and your problem, Will."

"Has she agreed to see me?" I asked.

"More than that, my boy. She insists!"

It was the news I'd waited for, yet I was suddenly terrified at the thought. "Tomorrow?" I asked.

"Lord, no! When the old crow insists, she gets what she wants at once. I'll take you down to her now."

My knees felt strangely weak and unwilling to carry the weight of my body. The fire felt scorching on my face, yet cold sweat was trickling down my back. "Now?" I said.

Sir Robert stuck his fists on his waist and looked at me. "Would you rather go home to be hanged as a witch?" he asked.

I looked at him seriously. "Yes, I think I would, if you don't mind."

"And would you like to stand on the scaffold alongside your friend Meg and Widow Atkinson?" he asked.

I sighed. "No, Sir Robert. No."

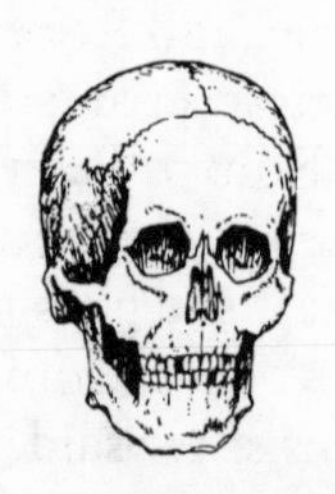

Chapter Thirteen

"I have seen a medicine that's able to breathe life into a stone"

I felt the way a criminal must feel as he walks to the gallows. My legs were weak, I was sick to the stomach, my mouth was as dry as the bones in Marsden churchyard. The corridors through the palace were dimly lit because the Queen didn't waste money on candles. The great chamber where her throne stood was even darker.

"The palace is filthy," Sir Robert muttered. "The servants are getting lazy because the Queen's too weak to control them."

Tapestries hung on the walls and covered most of the windows. Only the amber light of a blazing fire in a hearth at the side let me see that there was a figure on a raised chair at the far end. The room was hot and the air stale. "The Queen sits in darkness because she fears she is not as beautiful as she once was," Sir Robert Carey murmured.

Suddenly the figure at the far end of the room spoke. The voice was sharp, "Stop whispering in the presence of your queen, or I'll have your tongue torn out, Carey," it said.

Sir Robert laughed. "That would be a disaster. How could I tell you how beautiful you are if my tongue is lying in some muck hill, Your Majesty?" he asked, as we walked down the hall towards her.

The face was chalk-white with the lead make-up, the same that my grandmother used. The thick white paste filled in the scars from smallpox and the deep wrinkles of age, but if you got close you saw the ugly cracks. No wonder the Queen sat in half-light.

Her mouth hardly moved as she spoke. That would crack the lead paste and show her rotting black teeth, I knew. The orange-red wig glittered with jewels and framed the white mask-face as if she were portrait. Only the small black eyes looked alive and the fine, pale hands that were hooked like a falcon's claws. She moved one of the claws now.

"Come here, boy," she said. I knelt at her feet and scarcely dared to look up at her. Sir Robert gave a bow and stood comfortably at her side. Ladies-in-waiting at either side of her lowered their embroidery and looked at me curiously. But it was the Queen's black eyes that I felt cutting through me like the Thames wind. "What is your name?"

"William Marsden of Durham, Your Majesty."

"Ah, one of the Marsden traitors!" she said.

I raised my head sharply. “No, Your Majesty! We’ve always been loyal.”

“So you would argue with your queen, would you? It proves my point! Traitor.”

“No, Your Majesty,” I said miserably. This was going to be worse than I’d imagined.

“Sir Anthony Marsden fought against my grandfather, King Henry VII, at the Battle of Bosworth Field, didn’t he?”

“Yes, Your Majesty,” I admitted. Then I caught the eye of Sir Robert, who gave me a smile of encouragement. I remembered his advice. “But Sir Anthony was pardoned by your grandfather, Majesty. And my own grandfather fought for King Henry VIII against the Scots, my father fought against the Spaniards with Drake and my grandmother served you faithfully.”

“I know all that,” said the Queen. “How is Lady Eleanor? Still alive?”

“Alive but ill, Majesty.”

“Get off your knees, boy, and sit at my feet. Tell me about her.”

I moved to a stool at her right hand and sat there stiffly. “She has a chill, Your Majesty.”

The Queen coughed and the sound rattled deep inside her chest. “I have too. Has she taken no medicine?” she asked.

“There is a wise woman in the village,” I said, seeing my opportunity. “She mixes herbs and makes cures. But the poor woman had her cottage burned down by the Puritans and they are accusing her of witchcraft.”

“Puritans!” the Queen said in a grating voice. “As big a nuisance as the Catholics.”

“They want the wise woman hanged and they want me hanged alongside because I helped her.”

The Queen reached out a hand and placed it on my head. The hand was dry and hard. The nails were like

claws and it felt like the time Meg had dropped a lizard on my head for fun. I tried not to shudder as she rubbed my hair. "Never mind, William, you are safe enough in Richmond Palace."

"But I have a friend, Meg, and there is Widow Atkinson the wise woman. They'll be hanged if I don't take them a pardon."

"I don't want to know about your friend Meg," she said, the fingernails suddenly digging into my scalp. "You owe your devotion to your queen."

"Of course," I murmured, and the hand began its clumsy stroking again.

"I need a strong young man like you, William. I've been unwell," she said. Her voice was low and rattling in her throat.

"I'm sorry, Your Majesty."

"I will get better. I have my own alchemist working on a cure."

"Would that be Doctor John Dee, Majesty?" I asked.

The Queen stopped stroking my hair and looked around her. Suddenly she ordered her ladies-in-waiting to leave the chamber. "You too, Carey. Get out."

Sir Robert looked unhappy, but he stepped away from

the throne, bowed and followed the Queen's ladies through a side door. Only two guards stood at the main entrance. I was alone with the Queen of England.

"I need a strong young man. I'm finding it hard to walk since I've been ill. I need someone there at all times to give me their arm or their shoulder to rest on. A page, that's what I need. You will be my page."

"I need to return to Durham or Widow Atkinson will die," I said.

She brought her face closer to mine, and the stink of her breath and the warm spittle struck my face. "I am not *asking* you to be my page, I am *commanding* you. If you want a favour from your queen, you must earn it."

"Yes, Your Majesty," I said, feeling more afraid than I ever had in my life.

"You think life will be dull, serving an old woman, don't you?"

"No, Your Majesty," I lied.

"But I won't always be an old woman," she said softly. "Doctor Dee is a brilliant man. He has travelled all of Europe to find the Elixir of Life. Do you know what that is, William?" she asked.

"No, Your Majesty."

"It is the liquid that brings everlasting life. When I taste the Elixir it will keep me alive for ever, William. But it won't keep me alive as an old woman. Every minute I live I will start to grow younger. My hair is grey beneath this wig. It will grow as rich and red as it was when I was young. My old gums are sore and I can't chew meat as I used to. When I take the Elixir I will grow teeth as fresh and white as yours. And I will shed this wrinkled old skin like a snake and come out with a skin as fresh and pink as a rose petal. After twenty more years I will be young enough to marry a handsome young man like you, William Marsden."

It was magic and witchcraft more evil than anything Jane Atkinson had ever thought of. It was a dream that alchemists had had for thousands of years. The secret of life. Now Dee's studies and the Queen's wealth had made the dream come true. I only had one doubt. I remembered my father's story of John Dee and Edward Kelley. "Are you sure Dee can make the Elixir?" I asked.

"I have known him for fifty years and he has never let me down. He has taught me many of his magic secrets and I have seen the books. You can see for yourself, William Marsden. When you are not helping your queen, you can join the clever doctor in his workshop here in the palace. He is always complaining that he needs help. Imagine the reward! John Dee, William Marsden and Elizabeth Tudor can share the secret and live for ever. Would you like that, boy?"

I remembered the roses in the garden of Marsden Hall. I remembered Grandfather's wise words, "The old roses have to die and fall. That's so the new, fresh ones can break through. The old must die so the new can thrive."

"Remember," the Queen said, "this secret must be kept between you, me and Dee. Now go to that door and call Carey back into the chamber. He won't have gone far. He probably has his ear to the door at this moment." She gave a laugh that was a deep-throated cackle.

"What about the pardon for our witchcraft charges?" I asked.

The Queen's hand moved under my chin. I think she meant to tickle me, but her fingernail scratched me painfully. "If you betray me or let me down, William Marsden, then I will simply hand you over to the Puritans and let you hang by your soft young throat. You will help me. You will help John Dee. When the Elixir is made and starts to work, I will think about a pardon. Until then you can consider yourself under a sentence of death."

The Tudors had always ruled by terror. I knew that from the stories my family told. I would gladly have helped my queen if she had asked me. She didn't need to use threats, but she knew no other way.

I went to the door and called Sir Robert back into the dim chamber. He looked at me curiously. From behind the door he asked softly, "What did she want?"

"I – I can't say," I said.

He looked disappointed. He had been a friend and I had let him down. "I don't betray secrets," I said quickly. "I wouldn't tell the Queen that you have a great plan – you wouldn't want that, would you?"

He smiled. "No, William, you're right."

"Get in here, Carey, and stop whispering behind doors!" the Queen demanded and we went back into the gloomy hall. "Now take the boy to see John Dee in his room. Bring him back for supper tonight to serve me at table." She looked at me with those sharp black eyes. "Your grandfather once served my father with wine, you know."

"He told me the story," I said.

"The Marsden family have been loyal, as you say. Maybe now they'll start to get their just rewards," she said.

I bowed and Sir Robert led me out of her presence. The cool corridors felt fresh after the stale air of the Queen's throne room. Yesterday I'd have been worried about meeting the famous magician Dee. Now I knew he couldn't be any worse than his bullying, cruel queen.

His room was downstairs in a cellar. I knew we were getting near when I smelled a curious mixture of herbs and rotten flesh and something sharper that stung my nostrils. Sir Robert rapped on the door. "Who's there?" a voice asked.

"Doctor Dee? The Queen has sent the assistant you have been asking for."

There was the sound of sliding bolts and the heavy door creaked open. A white-bearded man looked through the small opening. A black skullcap covered his straggling hair. "Who are you?"

"William Marsden," I said. "You knew my grandmother, Lady Eleanor. And my father, Sir James Marsden, met you about fifteen years ago. He said you were a brilliant man and I'd learn a lot from you." It wasn't quite true, but I was learning that the way to live in Richmond Palace was to flatter and exaggerate.

"I don't remember," the man said.

"You were with a man called Kelley who spoke to spirits," I said.

The man's thin face closed as a painful memory passed through his mind. "Poor Edward," he sighed. "I've never met a scryer with his skill. I'll never replace him."

Dee opened the door a little. "Come in, boy. It's true I do need help."

I entered the room and Sir Robert tried to follow. "No, Carey!" Dee cried. "There are things in here not for the eyes of unbelievers."

"Hah!" the Queen's favourite laughed. "What'll you do, Dee? Turn me into a toad?"

"You're already that, Carey, so I don't have to," Dee snapped, and slammed the door before pushing the bolts firmly into place.

The room was hot because a charcoal fire was burning beneath a vessel. It bubbled noisily like boiling treacle. Some of the foul smoke missed the chimney and spilled into the room. The smell was overpowering. The doctor looked at me with wide brown eyes set in a parchment skin. "You are a brave boy, coming down here. Most of the palace youths keep away. They want to know what I do, but they refuse to help. They're too afraid of being charged with witchcraft," he said, as he stirred the pot with a ladle and sniffed at it.

"I'm already charged with witchcraft," I said.

John Dee turned slowly and looked at me closely as if he had a new interest. "That's good, boy. What do you know of the magic arts?"

I closed my eyes and tried to picture the book upstairs in Carey's library. "I know what the plant wolfsbane can do when it's mixed with human fat and soot."

He frowned, annoyed. "The fat is just to make a grease and the soot is just colouring," he said. "But the wolfsbane gives you dreams and in those dreams you almost think you're flying. Have you ever tried it?"

"No!" I said quickly.

"What else do you know, boy? Can you read the stars and foretell the future?"

"No."

"And what were you charged with?"

I couldn't tell him I simply helped an old woman escape from her tormentors. "Looking into a black mirror and trying to talk to spirits."

Now Dee was really interested. "Did you succeed?"

"There's something there, Doctor Dee, but I haven't the skill to make out what she is saying."

"Who?"

"The spirit. I think it's a girl. She is trying to tell me her name. I think it begins with the letter "M'."

"Madini! My old friend Madini! I thought she was lost for ever when Edward Kelley left. Where is this black mirror now?" he asked.

"In my pocket," I said, pulling out Meg's smooth-face piece of coal with the etched picture of Marsden Hall.

"Ah, the wisdom we can learn from speaking with the spirits," Dee cried.

"But what if Madini is a devil or sent by Satan?"

"She's not," said Dee. He stirred at the sticky mixture in the pot, but was too unsettled to give it his full attention.

"What do I get if I help you speak to Madini?" I asked.

"You are interested in gold like Kelley, I suppose."

"No," I said. "I simply want the secret of the Elixir of Life."

"How do you know about that?" he asked.

"The Queen herself told me."

"Then you are indeed a trusted one. I have been working on this all my life. Now I am close to the answer. I have all the ingredients here," said Dee, waving a hand around the room. It was cluttered with boxes and jars and books and bowls, and in the corner there was even a coffin. "All I need is someone to help with the mixing."

"Will it work?" I asked.

"There is no doubt at all about it. I have old manuscripts written in Greek that describe the effects. I believe that somewhere in Greece there are alchemists who are two thousand years old or more. The Greeks stole the idea from the Egyptians, of course, and they were artists at preserving life. Have you ever heard of a thing called a mummy?"

"No, what is it?"

"The Egyptians built huge stone pyramids that were supposed to be the tombs of their kings. But when the King lay dying, his doctor came to him and gave him the Elixir of Life. The King was wrapped in bandages, which formed a hard covering like an eggshell. Then a young, fresh body would grow inside the bandages and the shell would be peeled away. The young, fresh body would live on. That shell is what alchemists call a *mummy*. They would bury the mummy with a store of the King's fortune."

"Why would they do that? Why bury this 'mummy' thing? Why not just throw it away?" I asked.

"Because the doctors and magicians didn't want the ordinary people to know they had the secret of everlasting life. Everyone would want it! There would be riots and the King would be murdered. The King had to *appear* to die, then he'd reappear as the heir to the throne. But there had to be a funeral."

It sounded believable though remarkable. "Can you prove this?"

"Have you never seen a caterpillar? It grows old and dies and wraps itself in a silken shroud. The shroud goes hard and what comes out?"

"A butterfly," I said.

"Exactly! Caterpillars have the secret of everlasting life. The Egyptians copied the caterpillar and I will copy the Egyptians! Look inside that coffin," he said.

The last thing in the world I wanted to do was look inside a coffin, but I crossed the room into the shadowy corner. The coffin was standing upright and as I touched it I realized it was made of carved stone. I grasped the lid and pulled it open.

Chapter Fourteen

"Where death and danger dog the heels"

The figure inside was worse than the spirits that appear in your nightmares. It was a shrivelled, dark-brown body that stared out at me. I almost cried out.

"It came from Egypt last week. It is the shell I told you about," said Doctor John Dee. "The most powerful and magical substance on this earth. That mummy has what we need to make the Elixir."

I had a gruesome picture in my mind of Queen Elizabeth putting pieces of the mummy in her toothless mouth and sucking at it. "How do you use it?" I asked.

"We grind it to a powder. Then we take the only liquid that dissolves gold – a stuff called aqua regia. I had some sent from France last week," he said, holding up a small glass bottle. "Gold is the purest substance on earth. It is the gold that works the miracle in the body."

"Where do caterpillars get gold from?" I asked.

He looked annoyed. "We do not have *all* the answers. Men grow wiser as they grow older. Just when they are getting really wise they die! Now, with everlasting life, there is no end to a man's wisdom."

"Or a woman's?" I reminded him.

"The Queen has been my pupil for many years. Together we will defeat our greatest and most ancient enemy."

"The Spanish?" I asked.

His mouth twisted in disgust. "I am talking about the enemy of mankind. Not just of the English!"

"The Devil?"

"No. His servant. The creature men call 'Death'. Her Majesty is a brilliant ruler, but she will be remembered as the queen who gave her people the greatest gift of all. The gift of life."

There was a hammering on the door. "Will? Will Marsden?" Sir Robert Carey called.

"Yes?"

"It's time to prepare for tonight's supper. You have a few things to learn if you are going to serve the Queen."

I looked at Dee. He nodded his head sharply. "Tomorrow we make the Elixir and the Queen can have the honour of trying it. You can go now."

I unfastened the bolts and walked out into the clearer air of the corridor. "What have you been up to, young Will?" Sir Robert asked.

"The great secret," I said.

It might have been better if I had told him about Dee's plan, but I remembered what he'd said about the Egyptians keeping the Elixir secret from the people.

For the rest of the afternoon I was taught how to wait on the Queen. How to pour her wine and make sure her goblet was always full. The great chamber was filled with a small army of servants, directed by Elizabeth's Keeper of the House, a stern steward who ordered the men and women around mercilessly.

Tables were erected and covered in white linen. Napkins were folded expertly so they took the shapes of animals and birds.

A silver salt holder in the shape of a fantastic castle took its place at the head of the table while golden goblets, spoons and knives were placed on the cloth.

Ladies-in-waiting prepared the Queen's seat at the table with a canopy of silver cloth so she would sit surrounded by her wealth and dazzle her guests. Entertainers arrived and began to set up their performing space at the end of the hall where the Queen would have a clear view, and there was a dreadful din as the rival groups of musicians tuned their instruments and practised.

"Come back to our apartments," Sir Robert said. "Change your suit and wash the stink of Dee's filthy pit out of your hair."

I followed him through the maze of corridors, sure I'd never learn my way around this building. We climbed the stairs to his room and met Philadelphia coming out. "Ah! There you are, William. I'm glad I've found you. You have a visitor. I have to go and help the Queen dress for supper. I'll leave you to talk."

"Who is it?" I asked.

Her blue eyes sparkled. "A friend. But don't let the Queen know or she'll be upset," she said and disappeared down the stairs.

Sir Robert opened the door to his sister's withdrawing chamber and said, "I'll leave to talk to your guest alone."

He closed the door behind me and I looked towards the window. The wintry afternoon light was fading now, but the candles hadn't been lit. I saw her sitting at the window seat and she was the warmest thing in the palace. "Hello, Will," she said quietly.

"Hello, Meg! What are you doing here?"

Her back stiffened. "Aren't you pleased to see me?"

"Of course I am," I said, and took a seat beside her. "There's so much happening."

"Have you got our pardon from the Queen?"

"No. Not yet. But I'm very close to her. She's given me a job as her page."

Meg gave a smile as faint as the light outside. "So, you won't be coming back to Marsden to see Jane Atkinson hang?"

"Of course I will . . . I mean, no! She won't hang."

"She will if you don't get us that pardon. She comes to trial in four weeks' time. If she's found guilty they'll come for me next. I suppose you won't go back even to see me on the gallows?"

"Stop it, Meg! I'm doing my best."

"I'll remember that when they put the rope round my throat," she said softly. "I suppose you're safe enough in here?"

"Meg," I said miserably. "It will be fine. Trust me."

She looked at me, her sea-green eyes cold. "Why should I? You came here to fight for us and instead you've let the Queen turn you against your old friends. Remember your grandmother's stories about Queen Elizabeth? She's spoilt and cruel and always gets what she wants. And now she's got you! Your grandmother wasted her precious breath warning you."

"What do you want me to do?" I asked helplessly.

"Stand up to the old crow," said Meg.

I turned my face from the dying light so she couldn't see

my despair. "All right," I said. "I'll try."

She raised one fine eyebrow as if she doubted me. "Try?"

I shook my head angrily. "I *will* do it!" I said.

She relaxed a little. "Thank you," she said. "But you only have three weeks."

"I thought you said four."

"It will take a week for the pardon to be delivered to Durham," she reminded me.

"Of course. Three weeks – at the longest," I promised. I was desperate to change the subject. "You've brought news from the ship?" I asked. "How are things back in Durham?"

"Good and bad," she said. "Your father took his case to the Star Chamber and won, thanks to Sir Robert Carey's bribery. He's sailing back to Durham with the news. The Puritans will have to give back their part of Bournmoor Woods. Calvin Cartwright and his friends will be furious, of course. They'll stir up all the trouble they can for Widow Atkinson and for the Marsden family. I'm glad I'm working in the Mermaid, hundreds of miles out of their reach."

"Still, it's not really bad news," I said.

"No. I meant the bad news was about your grandmother. Your father called to see me before he left. It seems she's getting weaker. She spends most of the time sleeping. Her breathing is painful."

"But Widow Atkinson's remedies should be helping," I said.

Meg touched my hand. "Jane's wise and clever, but she's not a magician or a witch. She can't keep back death for ever," she said. I took her hand and squeezed it. "No one can do that," she went on. There were tears in her eyes.

"Perhaps they can," I told her.

I felt her hand stiffen in mine. "What do you mean, Will?"

I licked my lips which were suddenly dry. "Perhaps there

is someone who can discover the secret of endless life."

"No, Will. It's a dream. No one can do that."

"Perhaps Doctor Dee can," I said.

She thought about it for a moment, then squeezed my hand again. "The stories, Will. You have to remember your father's story. He said Dee was a fool."

"He said Dee was fooled by a trickster. But he also said the doctor was a brilliant man with a huge collection of books full of ancient wisdom. A lot of them are in the next room, Meg. I've seen them. Somewhere in those books there must be some secret cure that can help people like my grandmother."

She shook her head. "No, Will. I won't believe it till I see it."

"If I found an Elixir . . . if I made some. Would you take it to my grandmother and give it to her?"

"No, Will. It might make her worse."

"But if I'd *tried* it. If I'd seen it work on someone. Someone old and sick like Grandmother. Would you take it then?"

"There's no such thing," she said slowly. "But if you swore that there was, I would have to believe you, Will."

I gave a long sigh. "Thanks, Meg."

"Who would you try it on?" she asked.

"The Queen," I told her.

Meg's jaw dropped slightly. Then she half closed her eyes and thought about it. "Yes. That's good. If it kills the old crow, it'll serve her right and spare your grandmother. If it works, it could save your grandmother."

"Either way we've nothing to lose," I said.

She looked at me carefully and stood up. "That's not quite true, Will. I don't know what the punishment is for poisoning a queen, but I'm sure you'll find out the painful way if it goes wrong. You have a lot to lose, Will. You could lose your life."

"Thanks, Meg," I said, standing beside her.

She reached up a little and kissed me on the cheek. Then she backed away. "Sorry, Will, but you smell dreadful! Have you been sleeping with a dead cat for a pillow?"

I smiled. "I was just about to wash. I'm serving the Queen at supper."

"Then I hope her cold is in her nose," she said.

We were laughing when Philadelphia tapped on the door and reminded me it was time I was getting ready. "I'll be back in three weeks for the pardon," Meg said. "That's the very latest we can leave it."

"I'll do my ... I mean I *will* get it!" I told her.

She left the room happily. I was going to miss her. But that evening I was too busy. I seemed to spend all my time running. I was sent for by a lady-in-waiting to escort the Queen into the great chamber. Guests were already in their places at the table. I had never seen so much rich material, priceless jewellery and brilliant colour in one place. A group of musicians had struck up to keep the guests entertained while they waited for the Queen.

In her private chamber the Queen sat in a dress that was stiff with jewels. Her wig was a brighter red, almost as crimson as her dress, and dripping with a hundred pearls. It was no wonder her frail body needed help to move her

into the dining chamber. The ruff was like a cartwheel, pushing her chin up and making her look down her fine nose at the world. Her face was as smooth a mask as the white lead could make it, with a juice made from crushed beetle shells to add pink to her cheeks.

"How do I look, William Marsden?" she asked.

"Magnificent, Your Majesty. Magnificent," I said.

Philadelphia smiled at me and held up a mirror for the Queen to take a final look. "Nature blessed me with my beauty," she said. "I cannot take the credit. Now, William, give me your arm."

I stood on her left and let her clawed hand grasp my wrist. I felt her slight weight, but she could not rise. Philadelphia moved quickly to her right and put a hand under her elbow. Together we got the Queen to her feet. Once there she took small shuffling steps toward the door. It seemed to take us an age to reach the great chamber.

"Who are our guests tonight?" the Queen asked as we paused at the door.

"Envoys from Scotland, Your Majesty," said Philadelphia.

"They will be disappointed to see me so well! King James would have rewarded them well if they had reported I was dying!" she said and gave a bitter laugh.

The chamber went silent once everyone had risen to their feet, and the music died as Queen Elizabeth entered. She walked slowly to her great canopied chair. One of her bishops said grace and the company sat down.

I hurried to the sideboards where the palace butler kept a selection of the finest wines and offered them to the Queen and her chief guests. First I took a sip from each one to test for poison.

The envoy from King James sat at Queen Elizabeth's right hand, but it was Sir Robert Carey, next to him, who spent most of the evening talking to him. The noise and the heat increased as the evening went on and I was sweating till my shirt stuck to my back. The wine-tasting was making my head ache.

The musicians took a rest and were replaced by acrobats and jugglers who threw one another dangerously close to the painted wooden ceiling, spinning and twisting through the air while the diners gasped, cheered and clapped.

The floor was cleared and the Queen invited some of her favourites to show their dancing skills for the Scottish visitors. Philadelphia and Robert Carey led the dancing before returning to the Queen's table for more wine. I caught just one snatch of the talk between Sir Robert and the sour-faced envoy as they stood behind the Queen's seat. The Scot said, "So what is the message?"

Sir Robert glanced at the Queen and leaned as close as their ruffs would allow. "Tell the King, it won't be long now."

The envoy turned to Philadelphia and took her hand. He bowed and kissed it. For a moment Philadelphia looked surprised. As the envoy stepped away she made a fist of the hand he had kissed. I was the only one who saw her open the fist, to reveal a ring. She tried it on several fingers before finding one that it fitted.

Sir Robert Carey had his great plan to make his fortune.

He'd told me it depended on the death of the Queen. Now I knew the ring had something to do with it.

While I was puzzling over it, Queen Elizabeth asked to be taken back to her room. I helped her to her feet, and we walked through the chamber while the dancing stopped and the diners stood in silence.

"Your bed is ready, Your Majesty," Philadelphia said.

"I don't want to go to bed. I never sleep. And one day I may never rise from it. Not if our Scottish friends have their way. They think they will get their little king on my throne, but they won't."

"James won't succeed you?" Robert Carey asked carefully.

"I will never name my successor, cousin Robert. Never! Not if they send a thousand envoys with a thousand gifts of tawny gloves and jewelled belts and silver-gilt goblets. The throne of England is not for sale for the price of a pair of gloves!" cried the Queen. The effort made her cough. Dust from the lead powder fell in a cloud from her face and it seemed to choke her and make the coughing worse.

Sir Robert found her a chair and his sister brought watered wine and took off the wide ruff. At last her fit of coughing ended, leaving her panting, her face haggard and frightened, the cracks looking like crushed eggshell.

"You must go to bed, Your Majesty," Philadelphia said, frowning.

The Queen didn't dare risk another outburst. She waved a hand weakly. "No," she croaked. "Cushions. Fetch me cushions from the window seats and the chairs."

Philadelphia didn't argue, but hurried off to pass on her mistress's orders. The Queen looked at me. "I am not well, William. But I'll get better again."

"You are strong, Your Majesty. It's just a cold," I told her, and remembered that it was "just" a cold that was killing my grandmother.

Philadelphia returned and began to whisper to me. "What's that?" the Queen said sharply. "Do not dare to whisper in the presence of your queen. I threatened to cut your brother's tongue out for doing it. What have you to say to William that's so secret?"

"If you please, Your Majesty, Doctor Dee has asked to see Master William."

"Hah!" the Queen gasped. "Go to him, William! He is our great hope! Go to him and give him all the help he needs."

"Help to do what?" Sir Robert asked.

"It's a secret," the Queen said. "And it's none of your business, cousin. You have your little secrets with the Scottish envoy – I saw you hiding in corners like the rats you are. Probably plotting to poison me, you worthless traitor, so James can take my throne."

Sir Robert smiled. "Perhaps we were plotting to poison James so *you* could take *his* throne!"

"It may come to that, cousin Robert. We'll see." She turned stiffly to me. "Run along to Dee's pit and see what he wants. If he needs anything, let me know. I won't be asleep."

I bowed and left her chamber as servants hurried through the corridors, carrying armfuls of cushions.

After spending hours on my feet, and with my head heavy with wine, I wanted to fall on those cushions and sleep for a week. But, like the Queen, sleep was something I would have to live without.

I tapped on Dee's door and the bolts slid back. "Come in, come in quickly. It's already close to midnight."

"Midnight?" I said, stupidly.

"The witching hour, my boy! The witching hour!"

Chapter Fifteen

"Dear sovereign, pardon to me"

"Witching?" I said. "So this *is* witchcraft?"

He shook his head. "It is not the force of the Devil that we are using. It is the force of the moon and stars. They control all human life and they affect the power of our potions. The Elixir of Life changes the person who drinks it. Midnight is the time of change between night and day. It must be mixed at midnight."

He looked across to the corner of the room. A fine clock stood there and showed a quarter of an hour to midnight. The slow ticking filled the room and it was like the sound of our heartbeats counting our lives away.

I hurried to obey the doctor's orders. While he measured two liquids into a pottery vessel he sent me to the mummy case in the corner. "We need two ounces of powdered mummy," he said.

"How do I make that?" I asked.

"Take a piece of the mummy and grind it in this bowl," he said.

"Take a piece? What piece?"

"A finger or a toe. It doesn't matter. Just snap it off."

I didn't want to touch the thing, but I made myself do it. The mummy was hard, dry and tough and it took some time to break off a finger and pound it to dust.

"Now, boy, this is where I need your help. We must mix all the ingredients at the same time as the clock strikes midnight. The powdered mummy, the aqua regia, the gold and the fresh blood."

"What fresh blood?" I asked.

"We need blood," he said impatiently. "Take your knife and cut a vein in your arm just as a barber would if he were bleeding you."

"Why can't we use your blood?" I asked.

"Because the potion will have more power if the blood comes from a healthy young man. You don't think I'd let a boy in on this secret if I didn't need him, do you?" He glared at me from under his thick brows and I guessed that if I didn't give my blood freely he would take it anyway – and not from my arm.

I rolled back my sleeve while he gathered the ingredients on the table. He placed a piece of gold in the pottery vessel and arranged the powdered mummy so that they didn't touch. He held the aqua regia over the bowl and looked at the clock that was creeping to the XII mark at the top.

"Cut your arm and let the blood run freely, but don't let it drop into the bowl until the clock strikes," he said.

I was glad I'd sharpened my knife on a whetstone before dinner. I jabbed at my forearm and judged it badly. There was far more blood than I meant to release. It streamed on to my fine new velvet suit while the clock ticked on and on.

The warmth I'd felt was replaced by shivering and my sleepiness became a strong desire to close my eyes and fall asleep on the stone floor. Then there was a whirring sound as the clock mechanism began to wind the striker back and hit the bell.

"Ready!" Dee cried.

I shook my head to clear it and felt sweat spray from my forehead. The clock struck. I moved my arm over the bowl and the blood struck the gold at the same moment as Dee's

yellowish liquid. He moved a glass rod quickly to stir in the mummy powder. "Enough!" he said as the clock finished striking twelve.

I staggered away from the table and wrapped a handkerchief around the wound. Doctor Dee was pouring the Elixir into a glass bottle. He put in a stopper and shook the mixture. Then he placed the bottle in a cupboard on the wall and locked it with a key from a collection at his belt.

"Tomorrow I present it to the Queen and my fortune is made," he said.

"And mine, Doctor Dee," I said. "After all, it's my blood in there."

"But it is I who made it," he said. "Now get out of here and remember ... say nothing to anyone."

I was glad to get out of the room and its evil smells. I climbed the stairs wearily till I was at the level of the great chamber. Servants were clearing the remains of the meal while the housekeeper was checking the gold and silver plate. Robert Carey entered from the Queen's chamber and walked beside me towards his tower. "She is lying on cushions and demands to be entertained by her ladies. If she's not going to sleep, her ladies will have to take it in turns to spend the nights with her."

We turned on to the stairway of the tower and I paused, gathering my strength for the climb. Sir Robert peered at me in the dim light of the candles. "Are you all right, Will? You look exhausted."

"The wine and the heat," I said.

"And a trip to Doctor Dee, of course. What did he want?"

"Just my blood," I said truthfully.

"Ah, one of those experiments. If cousin Elizabeth wasn't Queen, he'd have been hanged years ago."

"It's just alchemy, not witchcraft," I protested.

"The people of Mortlake don't believe that. They will break into his house and utterly destroy it one of these days. They are very angry. It's very hard to prove you're *not* a witch."

"I know," I said quietly.

"Of course you do! Sorry, Will, I'd forgotten your problem. Maybe I can help."

"Would you?"

He stopped at the door to his apartments while I leaned wearily against a cool stone wall. There were no fine panels in this part of the palace. "I think we can help one another, Will."

"How?"

His laughing grey eyes sparkled. "I know you Marsdens like stories, so here's one for you, Will. There was once a Roman emperor called Hadrian. He went to the baths one day and had his back scraped clean by a slave using a metal scraper. On his way out he saw one of his old soldiers, standing against a stone column, rubbing his back up and down. He asked the old man what he was doing and the soldier said he was too poor to afford a slave. The Emperor liked the old man so he gave him money to buy some slaves of his own. The next day Hadrian went back to the baths and they were full of old men rubbing their backs up and down the columns!"

I laughed in spite of my weariness.

"What do you imagine Hadrian did?"

"Gave them all money?"

"No, that would have been foolish. He simply spoke to the old men and said it would be a really good idea if they arranged to take turns to scrape one another's backs. Then he left them to get on with it."

"We usually tell stories for a reason at Marsden Hall," I said.

"And so do I," he said, smiling. "Our emperor is Elizabeth and she is too mean to help us. So we must help one another. I will scrape your back if you will scrape mine."

"What do you want me to do?" I asked.

"Tell me Dee's great secret."

I closed my eyes for a few moments then looked at him. "And in return you will tell me your great secret?"

"Hah!" he laughed. "No, Will, I can't do that. But I will help you get that pardon."

My mind was numb with tiredness, but I wasn't going to betray my queen that easily. "I have two weeks," I said. "If I don't get the pardon in two weeks, then all is lost. Ask me again in two weeks and I may have changed my mind. In two weeks my back may be desperately in need of scraping."

He bowed his head. "In the meantime I will use other means to find Dee's secret. When the future of England is at stake, I can't wait for you to make up your mind. I'll get to the truth by any road I can."

"So, we're enemies, Sir Robert?"

He laughed again and wrapped an arm around my shoulder. "No, Will, not enemies." He opened the apartment door. "I couldn't fight a young man who has such a deadly weapon."

"What weapon do I have?" I asked.

"You cloak yourself in a stink that would poison a dog at fifty paces!" He walked off to his room, chuckling happily at his joke.

I slipped off my bloodstained doublet and asked a manservant to have it cleaned and dried for me. I sank back on the swansdown mattress and hadn't the strength to pull the curtains around the bed before I fell asleep.

I was woken the next day by Philadelphia, who shook my shoulder. My arm burned with pain, my mouth tasted as if I'd chewed powdered mummy and an ache stabbed at the back of my eyes. I didn't want to be woken and I didn't want to get up.

"Doctor Dee is asking for you," Philadelphia said.

There were dark shadows beneath her red-rimmed eyes and her fine skin was as grey as the winter sky. She was exhausted from spending the night awake with the Queen.

"How is Her Majesty?" I asked.

"She fell asleep for two hours at about four o'clock, but her breathing is too fast and she is fevered. This may be her last illness," she said.

I washed in a bowl of cold water and tidied my hair with a fine comb. I put on one of my old doublets since it would only get polluted by the foul smell from Dee's room, and set off down the stairs. I called in at the kitchen for some bread and cheese, then went on to Dee's dungeon.

He had the bottle of Elixir on the table and was sniffing at it. "It's perfect," he said. "The Queen will start to recover the moment she tastes it."

He took a flagon from the floor. "I have measured one drop of Elixir into this pint of wine. The Queen – and no one else – must drink this today. I will prepare a fresh one every day. You are her wine taster and her server. You must only pretend to taste it and make sure Her Majesty drinks every last drop."

"What will happen?"

"After a week she will start to feel better. After a month we will probably need to mix another bottle. But you will see her looking younger by then. Take it to her now," he said. "And tell her it cost me twenty pounds to make. I need money to buy more aqua regia and gold."

I carried the flagon as if it were a glass butterfly. I tapped at the door to the Queen's apartment and was shocked when Sir Robert opened it. "Wine for the Queen. Give it to me." He stretched out a hand.

"No!" I said. "I have to give it to her myself."

"Is that so?" he said. "They say Doctor Dee went to the butler this morning and asked for a flagon of wine. Would this be the same one?"

"I've no idea."

"He may have poisoned it," Sir Robert said quietly. "I cannot let you give it to the Queen."

"I must," I said, and tried to keep the panic out of my voice.

He looked at me carefully. "I will ask the Queen what she thinks," he said, and disappeared into the darkened room

I heard her voice raised angrily and he appeared again a moment later. He shrugged, "It seems Her Majesty wishes to see you."

I entered the room and peered into the gloom. The Queen was in a night robe, covered by a blanket and lying back on a mound of cushions. "Come here, William Marsden!" she ordered. "And Robert Carey, you can get out and see to your friend, the Scottish envoy. Perhaps he would like a trip down the river Thames."

"It's freezing out there!" Sir Robert said.

"Then he'll probably catch a cold and die. It will serve him right for coming to London to spy on me."

Her favourite bowed and left the room. I carried the wine to where the Queen lay. Heavy tapestries shut out most of the light and what little crept through was cold and weak. The Queen had taken off her wig and her thin grey hair had been brushed and lay limply over her shoulders. The smallpox scars gave the skin on her face craters like the moon. "Is this Dee's Elixir?" she asked.

"There is just one drop of Elixir in this wine. You must drink it all, and the same amount every day."

"Bring me a goblet," she said, waving a claw at the table by the window.

I took it and filled it. She held it up to me. "Here's to your health, William Marsden," she said. "If this wine is poisoned and I die, then you and Dee will die the death of traitors. They will hang you by the neck, but cut you down before you are dead. Then my hangman will slice open your belly and throw your guts on a fire. If you are still alive after that, he will cut off your head and it will rest on London Bridge. The quarters of your body will decorate my favourite castles. Would you like to decorate London Bridge and four castles, William Marsden?"

"No, Your Majesty," I whispered.

"This is your last chance. Do you want me to drink it?"

They say some poisons freeze your muscles and stop your heart. But the first you know is when your throat freezes as you swallow it. That was how my throat felt at that moment. At last I managed to say, "Drink it, Your Majesty, and you will live for ever."

She kept her dark, heavy-lidded eyes on mine as she raised the goblet to her lips and swallowed the wine.

She held it out to be refilled, never blinking or moving her gaze from my face. "Is this Malmsey wine?" she asked.

"Yes, Your Majesty."

"The Duke of Clarence was executed in the Tower by being drowned in a barrel of this stuff," she said, chuckling.

"I've heard the story," I said.

"Let's hope I don't die of Malmsey wine."

"You won't," I said. "After a week you will be recovered. After two weeks you will start to feel younger and stronger."

"If that is so, then you will be richly rewarded," she promised. "You and Dee."

"He needs money now," I said. "He needs to buy ingredients for more Elixir."

She leaned forward and breathed her foul breath in my face. "Dee will be paid when it works and not before," she said, drinking the second cupful and holding the goblet out again.

When she had finished the last of the wine she lay back and closed her eyes. "Send my ladies-in-waiting to me," she said drowsily. "I do believe I feel sleepy."

"Perhaps the Elixir is working already," I said hopefully.

The black eyes opened and flashed at me. "You will know that if I wake up," she said. "And I want Dee to cast me a horoscope. I want to know what is going to happen."

I left her lying on her cushions and went back to Dee.

"No money?" he moaned. "No money! And you say the Elixir worked?"

"It seemed to make her want to sleep," I said. "She

asked you to cast her horoscope."

He nodded. "I had thought of that myself," he said. "I will need to use the books in Sir Robert Carey's library."

He took the bottle of Elixir from the table, put it in the cupboard and locked it. Then he opened the door and blew out the candle, leaving the room in darkness. He chose a large key and locked the door behind him.

Every day followed the same pattern. I took the Queen her Elixir each morning and Dee spent the day with his books. The Queen was well enough to dine in the great chamber most nights and I served her there, along with her chief guests.

On the fourteenth morning, after the Queen had finished her Elixir, she said, "I do believe I am getting stronger, William."

"Your Majesty – half the Elixir is gone. Dee will need to make more soon. Can he be rewarded?" I asked.

"And what about William Marsden?" she asked. "What does he want for a reward?"

"Only a pardon for Jane Atkinson, Meg Lumley and myself from the charges of witchcraft," I said.

"You can write?"

"Yes, Your Majesty."

"Bring writing materials. Write out the pardon, then bring it to me and I will sign it and place my seal on it."

"Thank you, Your Majesty," I said, and hurried to obey.

Half an hour later I was clutching the pardon I'd waited and worked for. That half hour meant I was later than usual in returning to Sir Robert's apartment.

I didn't know how important that half hour was going to be. Important for everyone.

Chapter Sixteen

"And she is dead"

Meg was waiting in the apartment as I knew she would be. Philadelphia had sent her word at the Mermaid when she knew I had been sent for writing materials. "I have the pardon! I told you I'd do it!"

I was disappointed that her smile was so faint. "Good," she said. "The *Hawk* is unloading now. Your father can take it with him when he sails north tomorrow."

"Aren't you happy?" I asked.

She turned her green eyes towards me. They were damp. "Your father brought news of your grandmother. She is close to death. It would be sad if we saved Widow Atkinson, but lost your grandmother."

"It would," I agreed. "But how would you feel if I saved Widow Atkinson *and* my grandmother?"

"Not even Jane Atkinson's skills can save her," she sighed.

"No, but perhaps Doctor Dee's skill can." Then I told her the secret of the Elixir.

"And it works?"

"The Queen seems better after just two weeks," I said.

"And you can make it yourself?"

"I can't *make* it, but I can *take* it," I said. "There is a half bottle left in Dee's room. If we take half, it will save my grandmother. Next time Dee makes a fresh supply, I'll take half and send it north."

Meg looked thoughtful. "Dee trusts you with his keys?"

"No. But he is usually in the library at this time. If I can borrow them ..."

"Steal them?"

"Very well, steal them. I know where the Elixir is kept."

Meg's misery was lifting as the morning mist rises with the warmth of the spring sunshine. The idea of doing something so daring as to steal from a magician excited her. "Can I help?"

"Would I try it without you?"

"You might try it ... but you wouldn't succeed," she said, grinning.

I explained the plan quickly and a minute later we were standing at the door to the library. I walked in boldly. "Good morning, Doctor Dee!" I said.

He put down his quill pen and scowled at me. "Why must I suffer being interrupted?"

"I need a book," I said brightly, and walked past his desk as Meg slipped in through the open door.

"Sir Robert has blundered in twice. Now you! What is wrong with you all this morning?"

I reached for one of the largest books I could find, pulled it off the shelf and swayed dangerously towards the doctor. He rose to his feet to help me. "Careful!" he cried. "That is one of my books and it's priceless!"

"Sorry," I gasped. "Can you help me put it back?"

With my clumsiness it took us a full minute to replace the book. "What do you want?" Dee snapped.

"A book of poetry to read to the queen. Lady Carey said it was here somewhere. I'll ask her where she put it," I said, and hurried out of the door. Meg was already outside. "You have them?" I asked. She nodded and waved Dee's key ring at me.

We hurried through the palace and down to Dee's room. I'd seen him open it often enough to know which keys fitted the locks. I didn't light a candle, but worked in the faint light that came through the doorway. I took an empty bottle and poured in half of the Elixir. I replaced the Elixir on the shelf and left, locking the cupboard and the room.

I gave Meg instructions as we climbed up and went to the courtyard door. "Better give her double the strength until she begins to recover," I said.

The daylight was bright enough to make me blink. Spring was coming to London and I hadn't noticed, I'd spent so much time in the gloom of the palace. A southwest breeze blew the stench of Dee's workshop out of my clothes and it would blow Meg and my father safely back to Wearmouth. I had a sudden wish to be with them.

Meg put the Elixir and the pardon safely inside a pocket in her dress before mounting the old mare she'd borrowed from the Mermaid. She rode off happily and left a small emptiness inside me.

I ran up the tower stairs and back to the library. "Sorry to disturb you again, Doctor Dee," I said, as I threw open the door. I managed to knock his robe from its hanger on the back of the door and as I swept it up I hooked the keys back on to the belt.

"You're as clumsy as Carey!" snapped Dee. "He did the same thing. That robe will be ruined!"

"Sorry," I said, brushing it quickly. I took a book of poems and left the doctor to his studies.

Sir Robert was in the withdrawing chamber with his sister. I heard the word "ring" and stopped outside with the door ajar. "You're exhausted," Sir Robert was saying. "But now that I've dealt with it you should be all right. There's not much longer to go now."

I coughed and pushed open the door. "Good morning," I said brightly.

Sir Robert looked round quickly. He was smiling happily. Philadelphia was weary and grey-faced. She toyed with a sapphire ring on her finger. She rose slowly and said, "I'm off to bed. Excuse me, Will."

I watched her go. "How is the great plan going?" I asked Sir Robert.

"Hah! Better than yours, Will, better than yours."

He would say no more, but, whenever I saw him that day, he could not keep from smiling.

When I took the Queen's wine the following morning, Doctor Dee complained that the Elixir bottle was almost empty. "We'll have to make more within the week."

I said nothing, but took the wine to the Queen as usual. "It's strangely bitter this morning, William Marsden. Has Dee changed the Elixir?" she complained.

"No, Your Majesty. He is near the end of the bottle. Wine goes sour when you get to the dregs at the bottom. Perhaps the Elixir is the same."

That day she slept deeply. It was difficult to wake her for supper and she refused to eat. She slept the night away and word went around the palace that she was losing her battle to stay alive. The next morning I managed to get her to drink most of the wine, but it seemed to make her worse. The great chamber outside was filled with frowning ministers instead of musicians and dancers. They muttered quietly as messengers scurried to and from the palace.

In the evening Sir Robert came to the door of the great chamber. Twenty grey-haired, black-robed men turned

towards him. “The Queen is awake,” Sir Robert told them. “She wishes to see her chief ministers.”

“How is she?” asked a small, round-shouldered man. I knew that was her chief minister, Cecil – the one she called Pygmy.

“Dying as sure as the light at the end of the day,” her favourite said mournfully.

“She has had a fine bright reign,” Cecil said. “Has she named the one who’ll take her throne?”

“Not yet,” Sir Robert said. “Perhaps when she sees you gathering like crows around a dying sheep she will change her mind. Will you follow me, my lords and gentlemen?”

They trooped silently into the Queen’s chamber. She had insisted on being dressed in her finest white gown, studded with blood-red rubies. A man was bent over her hand. “That’s her jeweller,” Sir Robert murmured. “Her hand has swollen and he’s having to cut the ring from her finger.”

The jeweller stood up with the ring in his hand and the Queen gave a great sigh. “My coronation ring,” she cried. “My hand has never worn a wedding ring . . . I was married to England with that ring . . . and now I am divorced.”

She lay back on her cushions and the heavy, jewelled wig dragged her head back awkwardly. No one moved so I hurried to her side to support her head. “Have you the

Elixir, William?" she whispered.

"Yes, Your Majesty."

Secretary Cecil stepped forward and said, "We all hope Your Majesty will recover. But if by some tragedy you were to die, your beloved England would be lost. Your people would love you more if you would name the one who will take the crown."

She began murmuring and Cecil stepped closer to catch her words. I held her head as he bent forward so only he and I heard those words. "I am not ... not going to die," she murmured.

The Queen closed her eyes, exhausted by the effort. Cecil gave me a warning look that I didn't quite understand until he returned to the Queen's ministers. He spoke in a low voice, but I heard him clearly when he said, "Queen Elizabeth has named James Stuart of Scotland."

There was an excited murmuring amongst the men and a great relief too. Sir Robert ushered them out of the chamber and I helped to make the Queen comfortable on the pillows. Cecil looked at me with hard, dark eyes. "You heard her name James Stuart, didn't you?"

"I heard her," I said.

He left the room as Sir Robert Carey returned. "It's all for the best," he said. "James Stuart is a strange man, but he's been a king since he was a year old and he will be good for England."

"The Queen isn't dead yet," I reminded him.

"Not dead, but dying," her favourite said. "I will be surprised if she sees the sun rise tomorrow. But stay with her, Will Marsden. I'll send Philadelphia after supper tonight if the Queen is still breathing."

There was nothing I could do for the Queen but sit there and hold her hand. Her ladies came and took off the heavy wig and dress while I had dinner. Then I returned to the chamber with a book and sat on the window seat. I pulled

the tapestry curtain aside a little so I had enough light to read by.

Below in the centre of the courtyard there were signs of spring and new life. A faint tinge of green as a black tree began to put out buds. Brilliant yellow daffodils, the flower of the Tudor homeland, Wales. Crocus flowers in royal purple pushed through the grass.

So much life outside while I sat in the midst of death. As night fell I dozed. I woke around midnight. Philadelphia and the Queen's ladies-in-waiting were in the room, talking among themselves. I rubbed my eyes and said, "What's happening?"

Philadelphia took a mirror from a table at the side of room and held it in front of the Queen's mouth. After a minute she took it away and looked at it by the light of a candle. There was no mist of life on the mirror.

"The Queen is dead," she said.

I was stunned. All our efforts with the Elixir had failed, just when it seemed to be working. I expected some sighing and sobbing from the women in the room. I didn't expect what happened next.

Philadelphia walked towards me, pulling the sapphire ring from her finger. But she didn't give the ring to me. Instead she leaned across and pulled at the window catch.

She opened the window and called down, "Robert?"

"Yes?" came Carey's voice.

"It's over. Here's the ring."

She passed it to his waiting hand. And suddenly I knew what Sir Robert Carey had done and saw his great plan. I saw everything so clearly it was as if someone had lit a lantern in my mind. I couldn't understand how I'd not seen it before. My mind must have been dulled by the gloom and fog of the palace.

I jumped from my seat and ran across the chamber. I stopped for a moment and looked at the lifeless form of the Queen – as dead as Dee's mummy. I knelt beside her, raised the cold hand to my lips – the fine hand she had been so proud of in her old age – and I kissed it. "Goodbye," I said. "I tried my best for you. I was as loyal as any Marsden."

Then I ran out of the chamber and through the palace. I leapt up the stairs to the Careys' apartment and into my room. I snatched at some of my spare clothes and crammed them into a bag. I took my riding cloak and threw it round my neck as I tumbled down the stairs. If I missed him by just one minute – one second – then all was lost. I crashed through doors where sleepy guards blinked and ran towards the stables.

The huge bay horse was being led out on to the cobbles and a second one was on a lead rein behind it. I snatched the rein from the groom.

"Stand aside, Will Marsden!" Sir Robert Carey hissed. The sapphire ring glinted on his finger in the moonlight and the spurs glittered on his heels.

"No. You're a murderer and I'll tell the world what you did!"

"She was dying anyway. Now step aside!" he said and reached for his sword.

"No. You already have one murder on your conscience. You'll surely go straight to Hell if you make it three."

"Who's the third?"

"My grandmother," I told him. "If I don't get back to her, she'll die and it will be your fault."

"What do you want, Will?"

"I want you to take me with you," I said. "I'll ride the spare horse."

"I need it in case my own goes lame," he complained, as the horses stamped in the chill air, impatient to be away. But not as impatient as Sir Robert Carey.

"You can always take the fastest horse," I said. "But you are taking me with you."

"Hurry, then. Hurry," he said.

I sprang into the saddle of the second horse and set off on the wildest, most impossible ride that anyone has ever made or ever will again.

CHAPTER SEVENTEEN

"Uncertain life and sure death"

The horse was the most powerful I'd ever ridden. Every stride swallowed the dark and muddy roads like a dragon devouring doves. So much power. Most of the time I rode behind Sir Robert Carey and had the dirt from his flying hooves flung in my face.

Sometimes we cut across wide commons and I was able to draw alongside. "Where do you hope to rest tonight?"

"Doncaster!" he called back.

"That's impossible!" I gasped, as the wind snatched the breath from my mouth. "It's a hundred and fifty miles!"

"One hundred and sixty-four, give or take a few yards. We have been planning this a long time," he cried.

The streets of London should have been empty at that time of night. But we reached a crossroads and a cart pulled out ahead of us. Sir Robert didn't even break his stride, but crouched and let the fine horse leap over the cart and its load. My own horse took the lead and followed. I bit my tongue with the jar of the landing and galloped after him.

"What was that?" I asked, as I drew alongside.

"A cart full of plague corpses. They bury them at night," he said.

"Plague? In spring?"

"The plague's come to London early this year. This is

the year for deaths," he said harshly and rushed on.

When we had passed the walls of London we suddenly rattled over a crude bridge of wooden planks. "They're building a big new ditch around the city," Carey slowed to explain.

"Why?"

"They're afraid the Scots will attack as soon as they hear of the Queen's death."

We left London far behind under its smoky sky. On some wild heath I think some robbers tried to stand in Sir Robert's way. I heard the cry of "Stand and deliver" but it was followed by a scream of rage and pain as his horse rode them down. I spurred my stallion on and saw the flash of gunpowder followed by the crack of a pistol. I waited for the stab of pain as the bullet hit me, but only heard the wild laughter of Sir Robert.

Slowly the moon sank in the west as the first faint light of a new dawn glowed in the east. We raced past the startled watchmen in St Albans and vanished into the town's largest tavern before they could stop and question us. "They know the plague's in London," Sir Robert said. "They won't welcome strangers from there."

As fresh horses were saddled and we ate breakfast, I was able to question Sir Robert Carey and get the story clear.

"Your great plan is to be first to Scotland with the news of Queen Elizabeth's death," I said.

"That's right. I've been sent on missions to King James before and we always got on well. We agreed that I would get the news to him as soon as possible so he could enter England at once. King James wants to take the throne before any of the other claimants are out of bed ... so to speak."

"And he's promised you a great reward for this?"

"I will have a position in King James's court even greater than I held in Queen Elizabeth's," he said.

"The sapphire ring is the sign that the Queen is dead?"

"That's right. And I have horses posted every twenty-five miles or so."

"That must have cost you a lot of money," I said. "The longer the Queen lived the more you had to pay to keep them stabled and fit and ready."

"That's right," he admitted.

"So you were keen to see the Queen die quickly. That's why you murdered her."

"No!" he cried. "You have it all wrong, Will."

"Two days ago you went into your library where Dee was working. You stole his keys and found the Elixir we were giving the Queen. You replaced it with poison. Then you returned the keys to Dee and the next day I fed the Queen your drug instead of the Elixir."

"The drug was a strong sleeping draught," Sir Robert said. "The Queen was exhausting my sister Philadelphia with all those sleepless nights. I didn't poison her."

"No, but you took away Dee's Elixir that was saving her."

Robert wiped his mouth with a napkin and leaned forward. "There is no such thing as an Elixir of Life, Will. It's just a witch's dream."

"The Queen was getting stronger," I said.

"That's how magic works. It works on people's minds. If I give you beetles stewed in toad's droppings and I tell you it will make you better . . . then you *feel* better. That's because you are happier. You believe the magic muck is working. It isn't really."

"Half an hour after you stole the Elixir, I stole the bottle myself and sent half of it to my grandmother. But she won't be drinking Dee's Elixir, will she? She'll be drinking your sleeping drug. It will kill her."

"It's harmless."

"It killed the Queen," I said. "It's heading up the North Sea right now to kill my grandmother."

"The Queen was dying," he said, spreading his hands. "The country has been dying for years. You don't let an old dog suffer in old age. You shoot it. It's a kindness."

I felt the blood rush to my face. "You can live with the death of your queen. But I shouldn't have to live with the thought that I murdered my own grandmother."

He held up a hand. "No, Will. You shouldn't have to live with that. I'm truly sorry. Perhaps we can stop it happening. When does your father's ship get back?"

"The wind is fresh and he's a good sailor. I guess they'll get to Wearmouth tomorrow afternoon and be in Marsden Hall by evening."

"We'll be in Durham around then. It will be a close thing, but you may make it." He pushed back his bench. "We need to use every minute of daylight if we're going to reach Doncaster tonight. I don't want to ride by moonlight if I can help it. Let's go."

I followed him, stiff and saddle-sore, but determined to win the race against my father's *Hawk*. The wind grew stronger throughout that day and swung to the west. It whipped our cloaks and showers of rain stung our faces, but I knew it would be slowing the ship and I didn't mind.

By afternoon I was exhausted. When we reached the flat lands around Peterborough the roads straightened. The rhythm of the drumming hooves almost sent me to sleep. Miles rolled by like a dream where I felt I was flying like a wild bird. Then the horse stumbled on a rut and flung me forwards, waking me from the daze.

Mileposts ticked by like Doctor Dee's clock, measuring the distance to Doncaster. After the last change of horses I counted almost every mile from twenty down to one. The showers cleared from the sky and gave us the last of the dying daylight for our ride through the streets of the city. The citizens moved out of our way and stared at us a little fearfully. We were mud-stained and red-eyed like two outlaw fugitives, so I can't blame them for avoiding us.

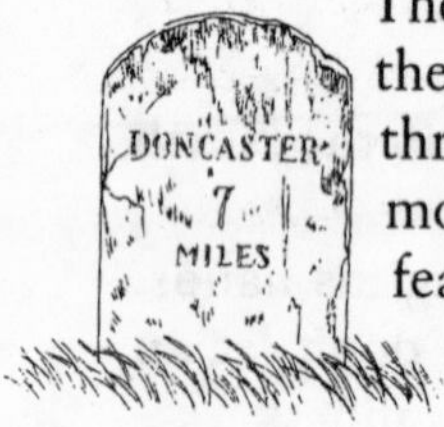

DONCASTER 7 MILES

I fell from the horse and staggered into the tavern. I collapsed on to the straw pallet bed and slept without chaning out of my riding clothes. Sir Robert was shaking me awake moments later, it seemed. "It's almost dawn," he said. "You've slept six hours. Let's change and get on the road again. The horses are ready."

The insides of my legs were raw where they had been gripping the saddle, my hands were bruised and too swollen to fit into my gloves. My back felt as if it had been

on the rack in the Tower of London. I crawled down the stairs, ate hungrily and felt refreshed enough to climb into the saddle.

The stiffness went, but the fresh clothes chafed and blistered me in new places. The insides of my knees were too tender to grip the saddle and the strongest horses raced away with me when they were fresh.

Then I started to recognize the countryside we were racing through. We breasted a hill and I saw the mighty tower of Durham Cathedral. It was just after noon and tears were in my eyes as I looked around the familiar marketplace and climbed down for my last change of horses.

Sir Robert was unshaven and the laughter in his eyes had died. "Keep this horse," he said. "I'll call at Marsden Manor on my way back south with the King."

"Thanks," I said.

"Have you much further to go?"

"A dozen miles. I'll leave you just after Chester-le-Street."

"Good luck, Will Marsden," he said, as I took the road that led through Bournmoor Woods.

"And good luck to you, Sir Robert," I said.

I wanted to walk slowly through the woods, look out for the deer and rabbits that I'd spent so long hunting when I was younger. But I was still racing against my father so I pushed the horse forward. I rode by Widow Atkinson's patch of land. The cottage had been replaced by a new one.

The village carpenter was fastening a new door on to its leather hinges, while a thatcher fastened new reeds into place. Some of the labourers were the ones who'd driven me and Meg from the village. They looked at me with guilt on their faces.

"Good day, Master Will," the thatcher called. "What's the news from London?"

"The Queen died yesterday," I said.

The men looked at one another fearfully. "The Scots will invade then?"

"I don't think so," I said. "But if they do, the men of Marsden will be ready for them."

"Who'll lead us?" the carpenter asked. "Sir Clifford and Sir George are too old. And your father's a sailor, not a soldier. Would you lead us, Master William?"

"Would you follow?" I asked.

They glanced at one another quickly. "We would."

"So I'm free of the witchcraft charge?"

The men laughed uneasily. "Your grandfather got that foolish milkmaid to confess to lying out of spite," a labourer said. "She told some tale of the Puritans digging up corpses in the graveyard. I think they decided to go and hunt witches in some other place. Somewhere easier. In

Marsden Manor we all stick together."

"What news of my grandmother?" I asked.

The men went silent and looked at the thin grass beneath their feet. At last the thatcher said, "Not good, Master William. Perhaps your father will tell you."

"He's home?" I cried.

"He passed the crossroads just a quarter of an hour ago with Miss Meg. He stopped just long enough to show us a piece of paper that he said was your pardon."

That explained why my persecutors had become more friendly. I knew a quarter of an hour was long enough for Meg to feed my grandmother the Elixir. I spurred my horse, and it jumped forward along the woodland track and we sped the last few hundred paces to Marsden Hall.

The servants greeted me as if I were a long-lost son returning to the family home. And there was something more in their looks. Respect, perhaps, and maybe a little concern. I thought it was concern for my exhausted state, but I soon found out it was something else.

I raced into the stable yard and slid down from the saddle. The old house had never looked so welcoming. Martin the Ostler took the strange horse from me and said, "Master William, have you ridden from Wearmouth?"

"No, from London. I left yesterday morning."

"That's not possible," he said, and I enjoyed the look of amazement on his face. It was an amazing feat.

"Where is my father?"

"Gone straight to your grandmother's room a quarter of an hour ago."

I limped towards the old oak door set in the stone wall. Before I reached it, the door opened. Meg came out followed by my mother and father. "Will?" my mother said. "How did you get home?"

"I rode with Sir Robert Carey. He's taking the news to Scotland. Queen Elizabeth is dead."

My father grabbed my shoulders. "Is she, by God? Then I'll have to raise a troop of soldiers from the manor. Guard against riots. Is James named as the next king?"

"Yes," I said.

"Then there are some who won't like that."

He strode across the lawn, calling for his horse. Meg and my mother looked at one another and then back at me. The late afternoon sun was warm here in the shelter of the Marsden garden walls.

"The Elixir, Meg!" I cried. "Has Grandmother taken the Elixir?"

She looked at my mother, uncertain.

"Sit down, Will," my mother said.

I walked back to one of the soft turf seats that faced the dead rose bushes and sank on to it wearily. Meg ran into the house and came out with a flagon of wine and a silver cup. It wasn't as grand as the Queen's jewelled goblets in Richmond, but it was mine and I was drinking it in my own home surrounded by the people I loved.

Meg sat next to me, her eyes filled with tears. My mother sat on the other side as I drank deeply. "Tell me you haven't given her the Elixir, Meg," I groaned.

Her voice was flat and helpless. The tears ran down her

cheeks. "Your grandmother is dead, Will," she said.

I closed my eyes. "And I killed her."

"What's that?"

"I killed her with the Elixir," I groaned.

Meg reached into her pocket and pulled out Dee's bottle. "I was too late. I never had the chance to give it to her."

"What?"

"Your grandmother died yesterday morning, about three hours after midnight," my mother said.

I shook my head. "That's the same time the Queen died."

"She went to sleep and never woke up. It was a peaceful way to go. Your grandfather is desolate. He and Uncle George are sitting in the hall talking. Just talking about the past. Telling the old stories over and over again as if it will bring her back," my mother said.

"It's the end of an age," Meg said.

"The end of the Tudor age," I said.

"That's the way of the world," my mother said. "The old die to make way for the young," she went on, looking at the rose bushes and seeing the pale new shoots. "We'll never see the likes of your grandmother or the old queen again."

Meg was strangely bitter. "They'll be buried and forgotten. We all will. So what is the point?"

That's when I looked around the mossy walls of the ancient house and had my great dream. "Some things last much longer," I said. "This house may still be here a thousand years from now."

"But people aren't houses," Meg said sighing.

"Their stories are," I told her. "If someone writes down the stories they can live forever – as long as there are people to read them."

"Who will write our stories, Will?" my mother asked.

I was tired, so tired. But tomorrow – or next week – I knew I'd be fit and strong again. Fit enough to face the task that only I could do. "I will, Mother. I'll write and tell the world about our family. I'll tell them all about the Tudors. It's a terrible story in places, but it would be worse if they were forgotten."

We sat there and remembered my grandmother. We each told our favourite story about her and laughed at some of the good ones. It was the best way to remember her. It was our way of showing respect.

When the shadows swallowed the garden and the evening grew cold we went into the house, into the warmth and the living, and we shut out the dying light.

Epilogue

My story is finished.

But you know that stories are never finished. Some characters go on living when the book has ended. Sometimes you wish you knew what happened to them after the book has been closed. That's usually another story for another time. But, briefly …

James Stuart took the English throne and ended hundreds of years of war and division between England and Scotland. The Scots didn't hurry south to settle old scores as we had feared – they seemed as tired of war and content with the peace as their English neighbours.

As for my family, they didn't outlast the dying queen for long. Grandfather was very old and the loss of his wife was too much for him. He died within a year and Great-Uncle George followed him to the family vault in Marsden churchyard not long after. Two old men of war found peace together at last.

The great shock was my father's disappearance. He loved the seas and became more adventurous, looking for new markets for our coal in France and even with the old enemy Spain. He sailed off late in the second year of James's reign. While the country was wild with tales of a powder plot by the Catholics against the King, we waited for my father to return through the autumn gales. He never did.

So I was the lord of Marsden Manor before I was

twenty. I gave up my life on the London stage and returned home to look after the farms, the mines, the ancient woods and the old house. With my mother's help the estate prospered. By the time I was twenty-five she was telling me it was time I took a wife. "You'll be old and die one day. You'll want a Marsden son to carry on the estate," she said.

In Master Shakespeare's romantic plays the young lord marries the faithful young woman who has stayed by his side through all the terrors and dangers of the world. Meg Lumley enjoyed the romantic plays of Master Shakespeare and believed people should live that way.

In the real world a rich landowner, like me, would *never* marry a peasant girl like Meg. But Meg Lumley did not understand the meaning of the word "never'.

Of course I married her. Wouldn't you?

The Historical Characters

[illegible] a strong character, and she needed to be [illegible] had [illegible] She [illegible] would have [illegible] She [illegible] proud of her appearance [illegible] even [illegible] She loved money and [illegible] constantly [illegible] with gifts. She gave very [illegible]

SIR ROBERT CAREY [illegible] He was [illegible] by James VI of Scotland [illegible] and [illegible] carried [illegible] [illegible] weeks of her life at Richmond Palace, but, as soon as she died, he made an awesome ride from London to Edinburgh [illegible] to be the first to bring James the news. [illegible] hoped this would earn him a good reward. It was a long time before he was given it.

[illegible] PHILADELPHIA [illegible] Sir Robert Carey's sister and cousin to Queen Elizabeth, whose grandmother was the sister of Anne Boleyn. She became a lady-in-waiting to the Queen. The story of her [illegible] Sir Robert for [illegible] Edinburgh is true.

The Historical Characters

ELIZABETH TUDOR (QUEEN ELIZABETH I OF ENGLAND) 1533 - 1603 A strong character and she needed to be to survive the struggles she faced. She could be hard on her enemies, but was also hard on herself. She refused to marry the men she loved because it would have been bad for England. She was vain and proud of her appearance – even after rotting teeth, thinning greying hair and smallpox scars ruined her looks. She loved money and expected everyone around her constantly to give her rich gifts. She gave very little in return.

SIR ROBERT CAREY c.1560 - 1639 A clever and energetic man who did a good job in keeping law and order on the Border with Scotland. He was liked by James VI of Scotland and often carried messages from Elizabeth. He became a favourite of Elizabeth and was with her in the last weeks of her life at Richmond Palace. But, as soon as she died, he made an awesome ride from London to Edinburgh in sixty hours to be the first to bring James the news. Carey hoped this would earn him a good reward. It was a long time before he was given it.

LADY PHILADELPHIA SCROPE Sir Robert's sister and cousin to Queen Elizabeth – her grandmother was the sister of Anne Boleyn. She became a lady-in-waiting to the Queen. The story of her passing the sapphire ring to Sir Robert for his ride to Edinburgh is true.

DOCTOR JOHN DEE 1527 – 1608 A brilliant mathematician who could be quite stupid at times. He always denied that he was a magician, but many of the books in his huge library were about magic. He spent all his own money on his experiments and he struggled to keep his wife and family. Elizabeth respected his work; she was his friend and his pupil although she didn't reward him very well. His greatest mistake was to be tricked by a fraudster, Edward Kelley. Kelley used Dee's crystals for talking to angels and they can still be seen in the British Museum today.

JAMES STUART (KING JAMES VI OF SCOTLAND AND I OF ENGLAND) 1566 – 1625 Scotland was a dangerous place when thirteen-month-old baby James became King. Many powerful lords fought to control him and the country. He survived through being a cunning and patient plotter. He earned the English throne the same way – never trying to threaten an invasion or showing anger against Elizabeth (who'd signed his mother's execution warrant). When Elizabeth died he was ready to move south to take the crown of the richer country. The Catholics expected him to be more merciful than Elizabeth, but he favoured the Puritan Protestants – especially after the Catholics tried to blow him up in the Gunpowder Plot.

The Time Trail

1533 Princess Elizabeth is born, the daughter of King Henry VIII and his second wife, Anne Boleyn.

1536 Anne Boleyn is executed for treason. Little Princess Elizabeth has seen very little of her so she won't miss her.

1547 Henry VIII dies and Elizabeth's younger half-brother is made King Edward VI because he is male. But he doesn't live long and …

1553 Edward dies and his eldest half-sister, Mary Tudor, takes the throne. She is a Catholic and tries to make England a Catholic country again. Mary is unpopular when she marries Spanish King Philip.

1554 Sir Thomas Wyatt leads a rebellion to replace Catholic Mary with her Protestant half-sister Elizabeth. Mary imprisons Elizabeth, but cannot prove she supported Wyatt.

1558 Mary dies and Elizabeth becomes Queen of England at last. Her astronomer, Doctor Dee, helps her to choose a good date for her coronation. She is a popular queen although …

1562 Elizabeth falls seriously ill. She recovers, but the English people would like to see her married so they will know who their next king will be.

1565 Elizabeth is faced with problems from extreme Puritans.

1566 Mary Queen of Scots has a son, James Stuart, but she is forced to flee Scotland and ...

1567 James becomes King James VI at the age of thirteen months while Mary Queen of Scots is kept locked up in England. After all, she does have a claim to the English throne and she is a Catholic.

1569–70 Elizabeth acts to crush a revolt of Catholic lords in the North of England.

1587 Mary Queen of Scots is caught plotting with English Catholics to murder Elizabeth. She is executed and her son, James VI of Scotland, should be King of England if Elizabeth dies childless. Elizabeth refuses to marry or to name James as her heir.

1588 Mary Tudor's widowed husband, Philip of Spain, sends the Armada to invade England. He fails and Elizabeth is more popular than ever.

1601 Elizabeth's latest favourite, the Earl of Essex, leads a rebellion and is executed. Sir Robert Carey becomes her new favourite at court. Sir Robert quietly makes plans behind Elizabeth's back to make sure James is handed the English crown when she dies.

1602 Elizabeth is frail and her death is expected soon. Astrologer Doctor Dee tells her to move palaces to Richmond where her health will improve, but he is wrong ...

1603 On 24 March at three am Queen Elizabeth dies, the last of the Tudor monarchs. James VI of Scotland comes south to take over. After all the fears of forty years, it is a peaceful change of power and the start of a new age – the Stuarts.

The Prince of Rags and Patches

A visitor comes to Marsden Manor, bearing letters from the dying Queen Elizabeth to James VI of Scotland.

A man lies dead in Bournmoor Woods – murdered.

And Will Marsden, aided and abetted by Meg the serving girl, sets out to find the killer.

Meanwhile Will is puzzling over the story of his Marsden ancestor who followed Richard II into battle, was mixed up in the mysterious deaths of the Princes in the Tower ... and whose meeting with a prince of rags and patches gives Will the clue he needs.

Two parallel stories of murder and intrigue, each building to a thrilling climax!

The King in Blood Red and Gold

When handsome, foppish Hugh Richmond turns up at Marsden Manor, claiming to be one of Queen Elizabeth's spies and asking for help, Will and his grandfather seize on the chance for adventure!

Riding north to Scotland, Grandfather tells Will he fought at the Battle of Flodden Field in the service of Henry VIII. Then as now, there were desperate skirmishes on the Borders between the English and the Scots Reivers – cattle thieves.

Neither of them realize quite what danger Hugh is leading them into ... and it seems that all their courage and quick wit will not get them out.

Luckily, Meg the serving girl is very clever ...

Two interwoven stories of battle and adventure, each as exciting as the other.

The Lady of Fire and Tears

A silver cup has been stolen from Marsden Hall and Meg the serving girl will hang for it.

Unless she agrees to spy on her friends at the Black Bull Tavern . . .

For loyal Meg it is a terrible dilemma. Her friend Will is desperate to save her. And Will's mother decides to tell them the story she has kept secret for so many years . . . how she herself, as a young lady-in-waiting, was forced to spy on Mary Queen of Scots.

Two stories of spies and double-dealing are brilliantly intertwined in a thrilling drama.

The Knight of Stars and Storms

The Marsden family are in desperate trouble. If they can't pay their debts, they will lose their home.

So Will and his father, Sir James – and Meg the serving girl who refuses to be left behind – set sail for London with a cargo of coal to sell, to save the family fortunes.

But someone is out to get them . . .

And it is only when Sir James recounts his adventures sailing the Pacific with Sir Francis Drake twenty-five years before that Will and Meg are able to work out a plan of action.

Pirates, spies and sea captains feature in a tale of nailbiting suspense and excitement.

The Lord of the Dreaming Globe

A man with one eye is trying to kill young Will Marsden.

All Will wants is to get to Stratford where Master William Shakespeare has promised him work, but somebody seems to think he has important information.

And when Master Shakespeare's daughter Judith is kidnapped, Will and his friend Mag discover that the world of the theatre is not what it seems. Ceratin actors are spying on their countrymen, on the orders of the Queen herself …

It takes Will's courage, Meg's ingenutiy, and the genius of Shakespeare himself to get out of the desperate plot they find themselves mixed up in.